JOURNEY INTO DARKNESS
(The Tales of Shakespeare – Book One)

by

Caroline Jones Lewis

CONTENTS

And so it begins …. A story of love and hate, of trust and betrayal – and more

Chapter One - Beginning

Sunday morning and the City streets were enjoying their usual weekend sleep-in on a damp and tranquil morning. The weather already held a hint of misty autumn, the temperature kind, the breeze only gentle and the leaves still clinging to the trees along the Embankment tinged with gold and yellow and brown. A calm rested upon the landscape. In the CID office at the Met, the officers on duty plodded through the mundane tasks of everyday criminality in a lull in the extraordinary. The atmosphere was ripe and ready for intrigue.

******

When the call came in, DCI Benedick Shakespeare was grateful for the diversion from the paperwork he'd been grappling with all morning.

"Thank God, some action at last, Mickey. Let's go."

DS Mickey Gray, jaded from a slight hangover and disgruntled that this was his weekend shift, grabbed his jacket from the back of his chair and fell into step with his boss.

"What's the story, sir?"

"A young woman's been found alive but unconscious south of the river. She was found by two young boys out bike-riding in the grounds of a derelict warehouse. Paramedics are on the scene already."

In the Sunday morning quiet, they sped in Shakespeare's car across the river to the scene where the two boys excitedly related their story.

"We wuz racin' an' I said to Ollie, bet I can get to the top before 'ya."

"Nah," he said. "No chance. I'll beat 'ya, no problem."

The boys raced on their bikes along the side of the old warehouse towards the wall that was the far boundary, sent out by their parents to burn off an after Sunday lunch energy excess. They were brothers, Ollie and Jake, only a year difference in their ages. Ollie, the eldest, was slightly ahead but his brother was gaining ground when suddenly Ollie squeezed the brakes with a screech at the sight ahead of him.
"'Ere, Jake. Look. Bloody 'ell. It's a body," he gasped, coming to a halt.
"Blimey. It's a woman. D'ya think she's dead?"
"Dunno. D'ya think I should touch 'er?"
"Na, I shouldn't. I'm gonna fetch Dad."
"Right. You go then. I'll stay 'ere and watch over 'er."
Jake spun his bike round and sped off back towards home. When he returned with his father, the man bent to feel the woman's forehead. It was cold and she was damp from the muggy autumnal air. He tried for a pulse and at first he thought he found one, then that he didn't, then he wasn't sure. He took his mobile 'phone from his pocket.
"Emergency. Which service do you require please?"
"Police and ambulance."
"Can you tell me what the problem is, please?"
"My boys have found a woman collapsed and unconscious."
"Is she alive? Can you feel a pulse or detect that she's breathing?"
"I'm not sure. I thought I felt a pulse but then I lost it."
"Right, sir. Can you tell me where you are please?"
He gave her the details.
"Police and ambulance are on their way, sir. Don't try to move her. If you have something you can put over her to keep her warm, that would help. Can you give me your details please?"
"Ollie, go 'ome and ask Mum for a blanket or somethin'. Be quick."

By the time the paramedics arrived, the boys and both their parents were hovering over the comatose body now cosseted under Jake's Spiderman duvet. Shakespeare and Mickey now added to the scene.

"Well done, boys. You did good. Now off you go home with your Mum and Dad and leave us to deal with this. OK?" Shakespeare's intervention was a disappointment.

"Can't we 'elp?"

"No, not now, lads. You've done your job. You did well but this is a job for the grown ups now. "

To unified calls of "Aaaagh!" the DCI held up the duvet, now replaced by a blanket.

"And who's duvet is this, then? Who's the Spiderman fan?"

"Me," called Jake.

"Well, you'd better take it with you, hadn't you? Can't have you cold in bed tonight."

He turned to the parents.

"Enjoying the drama, aren't they?"

The father nodded.

"Oh, aye. It's all bravado, though. Would've been a different story if she'd been dead. That would've really freaked 'em out. Thank God she's not, for all our sakes."

"Well, they did all the right things. Thanks for your help; and theirs. If you'd take the boys home now I'll send someone along later to take statements. DS Gray here will take your details and we'll be in touch."

"Will you let us know 'ow she's doin'?"

"We will. And thanks again."

Shakespeare turned to the paramedics.

"She *is* alive, I take it?"

"Yes, just about. I've found a pulse and we've put her on oxygen. Her vital signs are stable at the moment. Can't tell you any more right now. It's lucky for her the weather's warm for the time of year."

"So what do you think happened here, then?"

The paramedic pointed to the sloping roof above.

"Looks to me like she fell from that roof there. There's a bag lodged on the guttering, see?"

Shakespeare looked up and nodded.

"Any ID on her?"

Not that I've found. She's wearing a wedding ring, though. Should be a husband around somewhere.

Shakespeare looked up thoughtfully.

"Hopefully there'll be something in that bag there. We'll get it down once you've finished here."

"We're about ready to go. Just going to get her into the ambulance as carefully as possible. We'll be taking her to St Thomas's."

"Right. We'll see you there and I'll get a WPC to stay with her until she comes round."

"If she comes round. That's a nasty head wound she's got there. And there's something else I've noticed."

The paramedic lifted the blanket, carefully, not to let in cool air around her body.

"Look here. Her hands and wrists. Look at her ankles. These marks; they look like rope marks to me. Like she's been tied up. And her hands are all bloody with little cut marks as though she's somehow cut herself free. Seems to me there's a nasty story behind this one."

Walking back to the car, Shakespeare and Gray discussed the case.

"Nothing much we can do for the moment. We'll just have to wait and see if she comes round. Get Holly down to St Thomas's to sit with her. And we need a 'photo to put out to see if we can get an ID."

"Sir."

When the two men reached the station they found another case awaiting their attention.

"Two girls detained at Euston, sir. Suspected illegals. The Transport Police are waiting for someone to attend."

"Usual story – feast or famine. Well at least it means I can

7

dodge the paperwork a bit longer."

DS Gray grinned.

"Privilege of rank, sir - paperwork."

"Is that what you call it? Bane of my life, that's what I call it."
With PC Holly despatched to St Thomas's, they set off once
more.

At Euston the two women had been separated and waited in
adjoining interview rooms. Shakespeare peered through the
window into the first room, and flicked through the notes
already available. A young woman sat at the table nervously
clutching her bag. She was beautiful, strikingly so, but clearly
under stress.

"This one is apparently the older sister, Sofiya Albescu," an
officer told him, pointing to the photographs taken and printed
for the files. "The other girl is her younger sister, Anastasiya.
They say they're Romanian but have no passport or ID cards on
them."

"Do we have an interpreter to hand?"

"There's one on their way, sir. Should be with us any time
now."

"Well, we'll wait until they get here. We don't want anything
lost in translation, if you get my meaning. What's the story so
far?"

"We don't know much yet, sir. We haven't started to interview
them yet. Thought it best to wait for a senior officer. But the
story they gave was that they're just in the country to visit
friends in New Cross. No passports. No ID. When our chaps
pressed them, though, they said their ID was at the Hilton
Hotel. We checked with the hotel, of course, but as expected
they're not known there. Plucked the name of a hotel out of the
air, I dare say. No fallible explanation for why they're here. So
our guys brought them in. They seem more frightened than
aggressive. The younger one's quite tearful."

"Ok. Well, we'd better talk to the older girl first them. Where's
the sister?"

"She's here – next door."

Journey into Darkness

The men moved along the corridor and peered through the window into the second interview room. Anastasiya was slumped in her seat, a pretty girl but not as striking as her sister. Her skin looked blotched and clammy in her distress, her mascara smudged in dark patches around her eyes and her hair was wildly awry.

"Well, they may be illegal but they're certainly not hardened criminals, are they? They've been trafficked and are on the run from their traffickers, I'd say."

"Escaping a prostitution racket, probably."

It was Mickey speaking aloud.

"That's about the size of it, Sergeant"

They watched the girl for a moment, then Shakespeare spoke.

"Well, let's get a coffee while we're waiting for the interpreter, Mickey; being as we didn't have time back at the nick. My throat's as dry as chaff."

"Perhaps we should have waited in the office until it was all set up and ready, sir."

"What, and be stuck with that ruddy paperwork again? Not likely. When you rise to the giddy heights of DCI, Sergeant, you'll appreciate what I mean. This is turning into a much more interesting day. First an unidentified unconscious woman; now a potential trafficker to sniff out. If I have to be working instead of at home enjoying my Sunday roast with my nearest and dearest, at least give me something interesting to get my teeth into. Much more my kind of a working Sunday." He imagined the scene at home, the roast lamb on the table, his wife and son seated at the table in cheery conversation. He could almost catch the aroma, the roast meat and veg, the tang of the mint sauce, the meal that he was missing; and sighed. DCI Shakespeare enjoyed his food.

Mickey Gray was thoughtful. Another Sunday he would have been seeing his daughter, a luxury now he was a part time father; swings and roundabouts in the park and a visit to his mother for Sunday lunch. The mere recollection of his life outside of working hours caused a pain in his chest, a tense tightening of the muscles that made him catch his breath.

"It was strange," he thought, "how his body coped with almost anything in a work situation but was not so accommodating with his private life."

He cut his train of thought and brought his mind back to the present. He watched his boss thoughtfully as he stirred his coffee, the man reading the notes given to him, the story so far. A new man to the Met.

"So what's your story, then?" he wondered. "What brings you to the big city from out of town?"

"Any clues, sir?" he asked."

"No, nothing we haven't been told already. There's no point in speculating. We'll have time to do that once we've heard their story."

A wave from an officer in the canteen doorway told them the interpreter had arrived and all was ready.

"Right, Mickey. We're on."

Journey into Darkness

Chapter two

Five days earlier – Wednesday 10th September pm

In the gloom of the evening drizzle, officers from the Border
Agency waited in the shadows as the first of the lorries came
off the Dover ferry. Jamil waved it on with disinterest,
watching patiently in the stream of departing traffic until his
quarry came into sight. On his wave of instruction, an officer
stepped forward to intercept the lorry's path, his yellow
fluorescent jacket clearly visible in the headlights. He waved
the lorry into a layby at his side.
"Me?" the driver mouthed.
The officer nodded. The driver glanced anxiously in his mirror,
only too aware of his vulnerability.
"Christ," he muttered. "Bloody sniffer dogs."
Beckoned down by the officer, he dropped from his cab as the
other officers stepped forward, dogs at the ready.
"Go," Jamil instructed. "Be thorough."
The passengers would have no idea they had been sacrificed to
another cause, the money they had paid wasted, the future
promised reneged on, merely a decoy from a far more lucrative
cargo travelling behind. Jamil watched with satisfaction as the
vehicle in the lorry's wake passed without challenge. He turned
back to the job at hand. Revealed in the back of the lorry, the
illegal passengers slouched miserably against the side panels.
"Kurds," thought Jamil. "I spit on their godless gypsy souls."
The Kurds were dirty gypsies, a lesson learned at his mother's
knee. There was no understanding or compassion for the
displaced persons they had become. He had learned other
things as a child too; and skills not to be envied or aspired to
that would soon be brought into play. Jamil's agenda in life
was purely his own.

On board the vehicle disappearing into the distance, the driver,
too, smiled with satisfaction as he crossed the port boundary.
He joined the motorway to the capital, his objective also almost

achieved. Two hours down the motorway, he pulled into a small estate of industrial units and came to a halt outside the one furthest from the road. The metal shutters opened as if at his command and he backed the lorry safely into the building's floodlit interior. The shutters slid back down with a clatter as the driver climbed down from his cab. He was greeted by a group of two women and a man. A spokesman stepped forward.

"No problem?"

The driver shook his head.

"No problem," he replied. "The man did his job well. They'll be busy for hours dealing with the cargo on the other lorry." He grinned a toothy grin. The older of the two women took control.

"Let's get them moved then. They can use the toilets in the back and there are bottles of water and sandwiches on the table in the kitchen. No need to alarm them unduly. They'll find out soon enough what's ahead of them. Sapphire, bring them in."

The rear door of the lorry opened and several layers of benign consumables were unloaded to reveal a compartment behind and a ragtag huddle of young women, all young, maybe not even sixteen. They stirred and rubbed their eyes, blinded by the sudden light after the darkness of the journey and gasped in air, fresh and sweet to lungs that had breathed no more than the poorly ventilated atmosphere of the lorry for hours.

"Out," the driver instructed, reinforcing his instruction with a pointing hand. "You're in London now – where the streets are paved with gold," he added with a cackling chuckle and a knowing look to his co-conspirators.

"Who this man?" whispered one of the girls. "I not like him."

"Sssh, he will hear," came the response. "We not annoy these people."

They trailed forward and hobbled down from the lorry, dishevelled, uncertain of what lay ahead of them, the optimism for the future that had spurred them into making the journey shaky in the present reality. Smuggled into a strange country from Eastern Europe with only at best a limited knowledge of the language and no protection from the law in their illegality. The daunting challenge of their uncertain future was only now sinking in. The hefty payments for false documents and the uncomfortable transport offered them no guarantee of the rosy future their patrons had promised but they had put their trust in those glibly made promises and had no option now but to obey.

The group who had awaited their arrival eyed the girls critically as they tottered uncertainly towards the building. The girls were draped around the kitchen when another man arrived, a dark man of foreign extraction and a voice with an accent that betrayed his lineage. He cast his eyes over them one by one. Two were tall, slim dusky beauties even in their current unkempt state, another two were passably pretty and five had potential for improvement. The last was plain by anyone's standards. None of the clients would be interested in her. But for him she would be perfect; he had plans of his own. Jamil was well satisfied with the evening's arrivals.

He spoke to the girl briefly. Turning on his ample charm, he introduced himself just as Jamil and gleaned that her name was Mina. She had limited English but at least she had English.
"Do you know how to care for children?" he asked her.
She nodded.
"Yes. My brothers," she told him. "I care for them at home after mother dies."
"How old?"
"One three years now, one six years."
"How long since your mother died?"
"When last baby born."
"And you cared for the baby?"
Mina nodded.
"Who cares for them now?"
"Father has new wife," she replied.

He considered and watched her intently. She seemed genuine, answering honestly.

"She will do," he decided, "at least to begin with."

And she was disposable, unmissable, if the need arose.

"You will look after my son," he told her.

She made no objection. She knew her limitations, especially seeing the other girls she had travelled with who were beautiful and clever where she was not. And Jamil was an imposing figure. Standing six feet tall and broad-shouldered, he presented a natural air of authority.

"How many years?" she asked.

"Six months old. A baby."

Mina smiled. When he led her to his car she sank into the passenger seat without a word. He drove her to a small apartment he had rented in the Docklands, sparsely furnished but a veritable palace to Mina. The kitchen he had equipped with what he saw as necessities for his son but with little thought to any adult. He realised there would be more to buy. In the 'fridge were the essentials, milk, butter, eggs. There was bread in the cupboard.

"Are you hungry?"

Mina nodded.

"A little."

"What do you want to eat?"

Mina shrugged.

"What you have?"

"I will fetch something from the take-away. But quickly. They will be closing soon. Pizza?" he suggested. "Burgers?"

"Pizza," she replied with a smile.

"I will fetch it," he assured her. "I won't be long. You can look around the apartment. Your bedroom is through there."

When Jamil had left, Mina took her shabby bag into the bedroom. Her meagre belongings looked lost and insignificant in the space and she stood at the window looking out across the river in the darkness. Lights from the buildings along the bank opposite reflected in the water. They twinkled and blinked across the rippling tide, holding her gaze. It was not an unpleasant view but it was a million miles away from home. For just an instant panic rose inside her. What if this man were to abuse her? Imprison her? Murder her? No-one knew she was here. No-one. The other girls had gone. She could disappear without a trace, discarded into the muddy waters of the river below. But why should he do that? she asked herself. What reason would he have? He had given no sign that he was anything but genuine, a man needing someone to care for his son. She quelled her fear and set about settling in until Jamil arrived with the pizza. Then leaving her for the evening, he told her he would return tomorrow and that in the meantime she must remain in the apartment and answer the door to no-one.

"No-one, do you understand?"

She nodded.

"No-one," she repeated.

He left her to settle herself in front of the tv before retiring for a restless night, wondering quite what the dawn would bring.

******

Jamil's story

In the early morning hours, Jamil considered his options. It was now way past midnight and return home an unappealing prospect. Baby Hasan would be sleeping. He felt no other reason to return. He dreaded sleep, the return of the nightmares that pursued him in his slumber, then woke him sweating in the darkness. His sleep was riven with images from the past, of faceless women that disturbed his slumber, spectres holding him to ransom, a cackling laugh and voices calling him a useless brat. Looking down on his cowering body were eyes that were out to get him, two large, clear eyes that seemed to be enticing him and two sharp, dark eyes that he felt were probing his mind. And all around a great heat consumed him. He would wake with a start, sweating and disorientated in his bed.

15

As a ten year old he had lived with his widowed mother in a village rife with poverty and crime. A harridan of a woman addicted to the local brew, his mother had beaten him at will and derided him as a matter of routine. Along with his aunt she would taunt him at every opportunity. That last evening he had known there would be trouble.

Returning from school the stitching of one of his shoes had come adrift and the sole flapped open each time he lifted his foot, impeding his walk. When he entered the wooden hut that was home, his mother was sat in the kitchen with her sister and partner in crime. The two women were clearly already the worse for wear.

"You wretch," shouted his mother. "You do these things to torment me. Like I have money to spend on new shoes for a useless brat like you."

"No," he protested. "I didn't, really. It just happened. The shoes, they are old and I stumbled on the stones in the road so the ...."

"Old. Old," she shrieked. "You call them old. I paid good money for those shoes and you can't look after them," and she cuffed him hard across the head. His aunt laughed, a loud cackling laugh like a witch in a children's bedtime story that had terrified him as a small boy, read by a mother not yet consumed by the poison of drink. His aunt pitched in.

"Go on, belt him," she cried. "He's nothing but trouble, the little runt," and rising from her seat she joined her sister to set about hitting him until he managed to escape their blows and run to his room at the back of the hut. His aunt was a witch, he was convinced of it. He fell onto his bed sobbing and hungry and burning with humiliation. He hated his mother; he hated his aunt.

"I hate you. I hate you both. I wish you were dead."

A voice in his head told him that it would not be so difficult for his wish to come true. If they were gone, he could live on his own and do whatever he wished. It was an idea that appealed and the voice enticed and cajoled him.

At the front of their hut was a small room that served as an eating and sitting room to where his mother and aunt would retire in the evening. Despite the heat of the day, the nights could turn cold so they kept in the hut their only form of heating, an old and dilapidated oil heater unlikely to pass any health and safety inspection. Once before his mother had knocked it over when she was drunk, setting alight the threadbare rug on the floor. He had run to the door, shouting to the neighbours who had come and doused the flames before too much damage had been done. He had saved all their lives and their home. But the voice in his head asked the question. What if he had not? What then? He fetched a chunk of bread from the bread basket and sat on his bed eating while he formed a plan in his mind. The voice in his head helped him so that fuelled by his anger he wasted no time in putting his thoughts into action.

Darkness fell and by then his mother and his aunt were considerably inebriated, snoring audibly in their seats. He crept into the room and passed the sleeping women to bolt the front door. Then, with trembling hands, he placed the heater on the rug and struck a match to light the oil. Checking it was safely alight, he moved near to the window he had already opened and standing ready to make his escape he used the handle of a broom to knock over the heater. Wide-eyed he watched as the oil spilled onto the rug and flared into flame. He propped the broom against the wall, then checking that no-one was around outside to see, he climbed out of the window and dropped to the ground, pushing the window closed behind him. The dull thud of its closure caused the catch to fall into place. The hut was secure.

From behind a bush he watched the flames taking hold, heard the sounds, the shouts of alarm and the sound of running feet as villagers gathered. He turned and ran as fast as he could until

17

clear of the village boundary, breathless, carried by adrenalin to a lake that was a favourite spot. He crouched on the grass, calming his breathing, then sat legs outstretched at the edge of the gently lapping water. The gentle ebb and flow of the wind and the water calmed him. The voice had been right, he thought, and he was glad that he had listened. Resisting any urge to return to the scene of his crime, his body sank into exhaustion and drained of adrenalin, he fell into a heavy sleep.

The hut had burned rapidly, the two unconscious women oblivious of the dense, choking smoke that overcame them and the heat that charred their lungs and fried their brains. Despite the valiant efforts of villagers, there was no hope of their survival. The fire crackled and spat merrily until it was done. It was not until the last flame was doused that the extent of destruction was clear.

"Where's Jamil?" shouted one of the villagers. "There's no sign of Jamil here."

"I expect he'll be at the lake," said another. "He sleeps there sometimes. when his mother - well, you know."

The villagers nodded. They did know. They searched for him at the lake and found him in the early hours sleeping, curled on a lush patch of grass covered only by his shirt.

Taken in by another family in the village, life had been better for him from then on. No beatings, no abuse, though still hard and the nightmares that pursued him had been credited to distress at his loss rather than a guilt that no-one knew he carried. He continued his schooling but worked long hours out of school time in the family bakery to cover the cost of his keep. His body had healed, the bruises had faded, all but a scar on his neck, an old burn scar from a glancing maternal blow that had sent him sprawling against the hot surface of the range in the kitchen. Treated by a nurse in the village, the damage had been minimised by an unctuous concoction smeared liberally across the red and angry skin, but the scarring remained. Katya had run her fingers tenderly across the scar

one day and asked him the question.
"How did this happen?"
But Jamil would never say.

The rest of the body had healed with time but the mind had not.
The mind remained as scarred and angry as the skin below his
left ear. And the voice remained in control.
"You see. I told you it would be alright. Now you are alright."
Jamil agreed. And the voice became his trusted companion.

At the age of 15, he had met Meryem, two years his senior and
already experienced in the art of loving. A tall and handsome
youth, there were several girls he could have had but no, they
would not do. It was the challenge of Meryam that enticed
him. Seduced both physically and emotionally, he had
followed her like a puppy dog and succumbed to her every
whim.
"Will you marry me, Meryam? When we're older?" he had
asked her.

Meryam had laughed, a light, teasing laugh that implied his
proposal was of little consequence, a matter of amusement.
"Marry you, Jamil? When I marry it will be to a rich man who
can keep me in luxury. Are you going to be a rich man, Jamil
the baker's boy? When you are, come back and ask me then."
Her tone of derision was not lost on Jamil. For him the tide
had turned. From then on Meryam had distanced herself from
him, offering only excuses when he asked to be with her.
"I am busy today, Jamil. Maybe tomorrow," until
eventually she avoided seeing him at all. It turned his mind,
the love he thought he had found metamorphosing into hatred.
Meryam had never met her rich man. Meryam had met an
untimely and unexplained death And Jamil and his companion
had moved on. Still he hated his mother and he hated his aunt.
And now he counted all women the same; conniving, self-
serving and not to be trusted. The only way to beat them was
to get in first. When the spectres visited him in his dreams,

19

waking him in the hours of darkness, his companion would reassure him.

"Don't worry so, It's not your fault. These people were bad for you. You only did what you had to do."

Reassured he would lapse back into sleep.

******

On this early morning the adrenalin was still high after the night's events. Return home was not an appealing prospect. Baby Hasan would be sleeping and he had no other reason to return. With Mina installed he felt confident that his plan was taking shape well and the confidence boosted his natural arrogance. Checking his appearance in the mirror, he started the engine and drove to Soho and the brothel. Sadie, the Madam, let him in without delay. He had the pick of her girls whenever he wanted – for free. As the most essential UK link in the supply chain, she made sure he was well cared for.

"Jamil, what can we do for you today?" she asked.

"Did the girls arrive ok?"

"They did," she assured him. "A good consignment, Jamil."

"Are they all here?"

"No. These two have gone to Mayfair," and she placed two passports on the table in front of her. "Sapphire is settling them in."

Jamil took the two passports and studied the 'photos inside.

"The two dusky beauties," he thought. He almost salivated as he studied them, then pointed to the one that appealed most.

"I want her – first," he told Sadie. "I'll call you when."

Sadie nodded. She knew that Jamil liked to take the girls he wanted first, before they were on offer to the regular clients. She indulged his whim when she could - and lied when she could not.

"I guessed you'd like that one," she replied. "I'll see she awaits you. She should do well if she behaves herself. She'll be for the top drawer clients."

"And the others?"

"These two are here," and two more passports were added to the ones Jamil already held in his hands. "The rest went with Mac – all except one, that is. Too plain. But I think she came with you?"

Jamil ignored the question, ignored Sadie's curiosity and she did not ask further. It did not do to be nosey in their line of business. Aware was one thing – but nosey quite another.

"Good," said Jamil. "It's been a successful night, yes? Now, Sadie - get me Ebony. She pleases me."

Sadie left the room briefly, then returned with a key.

"She's in the Green Room," she told him handing him the key. "She's waiting for you with champagne. A little celebration for another successful evening."

Chapter Three

Thursday, 11th September

It was early morning by the time Jamil was ready to return home. He parked his car back in the lock-up and walked the short distance to the house. Katya was in the kitchen making coffee. She recognised the smell on him – the same woman as before. She said nothing.

"Where is Hasan?" he asked her.

"In his cot. I have just bathed him."

"First I have a shower. Then I want to see my son. You fetch him."

While Jamil showered away the smell of the night, Katya responded to the ringing of the 'phone. It was Len Hutton calling, Jamil's boss and he spoke with urgency.

"I know he had a late night but tell him he's needed here as soon as possible," he told her.

"I will tell him," Katya replied.

Down from his shower, Jamil received the message with a grunt. Then ignoring Katya further, he went to his son who was now gurgling in his baby seat. At the sight and sound of his father Hasan beamed a smile and flailed his legs and arms in excitement. Jamil bent to kiss the child on his forehead and crooned a greeting.

"Ah, you are happy to see Baba, yes?"

"What would you like for breakfast?" asked Katya.

Jamil thought for a moment.

"Eggs," he said. "Boiled. With toast, not burned this time. And make sure the eggs are soft."

He took Hasan from the chair and carried him through to the lounge.

In the kitchen, Katya took two eggs from the 'fridge and placed them on the cooker in a pan of warm water. Her hands shook a little as she worked, the memory of the last time still fresh in her mind. The eggs had not been soft, the toast had been tinged at the edges and not to Jami'sl liking.

"What is this muck you give me?" he had shouted, raising the toast and thrusting it before her eyes.

"I'm sorry, Jamil. I will do you some fresh."

"I don't have time. And the eggs – they are not soft like I told you. Can you do nothing right, you stupid woman?"

He had raised his hand and caught her across her face so hard her head had jolted sideways, knocking her off balance so she had to steady herself against the worktop behind. The split lip from his slap had taken days to heal and stung with every sip or bite and every lick of the tongue. Her spirit had flared momentarily, her survival instinct kicking in and an impulse to retaliate close to the surface, to show him she was not prepared to accept his bullying. But a sense of reason overtook her.

"Be careful. He's bigger than you. Stronger. It would only make matters worse. And he could take Hasan from you."

She had held her tongue. She would bide her time.

"I must get it right this time," she told herself; three minutes exactly, toast lightly brown. While the eggs bounced gently in the simmering water, she laid his place at the kitchen table. When Jamil returned and placed Hasan back in his chair, his breakfast was ready – two eggs softly boiled, the tops cut off by her trembling hand and lightly toasted bread that was evenly buttered. The meal passed without incident. Jamil's mind in any case was elsewhere, content in the knowledge that soon he would not have to bother with Katya at all. He left with an instruction to take Hasan to the park for one hour to get some air.

"But you speak to no-one – do you hear? I do not want my son mixing with just anyone."

Katya murmured a subservient response and Jamil left with no more said between them. The door closed behind him with a slam. She breathed a sigh of relief. She smiled at Hasan who was now falling asleep, too tired for his mother now that his father had left and sucking hard on a thumb firmly plugged between his plump, soft lips. Her heart swelled with a mixture of love and anguish.

******

Len's revelation back in the office sent Jamil's brain spinning. "The driver of the lorry you pulled in last night," he began. "He's made an allegation. Denies knowing the guys he brought in were illegals but reckons he was set up and it was an inside job. He says word is there was a group of illegals being brought in last night and we stopped the wrong lorry. We're checking out the documents now. Heard anything about this? Any other tip off?"

Jamil shook his head.

"It's not possible, surely," he blurted. "Why would they come in by lorry if they were genuine immigrants? And why would our contact tip us about them and not another consignment?"

His boss replied.

"The lorry driver reckons that the chaps in his lorry didn't have enough money for public transport. That they'd got as far as Calais and then were stuck. So he just brought them across the channel as a favour. He said they showed him passports with entry visas."

Jamil scoffed loudly.

"Entry visas! Forged no doubt. So he is saying they are not illegals, just hitch hikers?"

"That's about the size of it. Doesn't make sense, of course. He's just trying to avoid prosecution and a hefty fine. But what concerns me most is the allegation of insider involvement. I don't want to believe it but I can't ignore it either. I'll have to look into it. Until we have some answers there has to be total security. The contents of this conversation stay between us, Jamil. Within these four walls. Understand?"

Jamil nodded, relieved that he alone would be privy to the information that came to light. He played his part carefully. Taking note of the procedures his boss wished him to implement, he left their meeting and headed for the coffee lounge across the road.

He paid for a coffee at the counter, then moved across to a table in the corner, out of sight of the window. Breathing deeply he calmed his racing pulse. Taking a pay as you go mobile from his inside pocket, he pressed a number stored in the contacts and waited for the voice at the other end.

"Jamil, why are you ringing me? Did it not go well?"

"Not quite. We have a problem. Someone is talking."

He glanced around him watchfully.

"Wait - just a moment."

He checked around him that no-one was in earshot but the place was almost empty this early and the staff were chatting and laughing behind the counter. In a whispered voice he outlined the problem to his contact and agreement was reached that further movements should be suspended until the culprit was identified.

"But not for long," his contact insisted. "I have bills to pay. And people are waiting."

"Ok, ok. Not for long. I will let you know when."

Having calmed his initial fears, Jamil felt confident that he could contain the situation. Apart from his contact across the channel and Sadie, no-one knew his identity, his insider status guaranteeing his value to the entire operation and therefore his anonymity. Neither party would have any reason to disclose his name should the situation arise. Within his employment he felt in control. Len trusted him, of that he was sure. With Mina arrived and safely installed at the apartment, he saw nothing to deter him from proceeding with the plans already begun. He finished his coffee, his pulse now steady.

Taking the tube, he headed for the flat in the Docklands to check on the girl, calling at a supermarket on the way for food.

"Are you settled in?" he asked Mina, dropping the carrier bags on the kitchen worktop.

"Yes, thank you."

"I have brought you food. Is there anything else that you

need?"

She shook her head, but then, about to speak, hesitated, unsure of whether to go on.

"What is it?" he asked.

His manner seemed relaxed and friendly so she took a chance. "I would like go outside," she ventured. "To find my way. But I need key."

"Not yet. Give yourself more time to settle. Later I will bring my son to see you. We will talk about things, yes? Right now I'm busy so you stay here. You rest, watch tv or something."

Mina was disappointed but reluctant to disagree. This could be a good position for her and she looked forward to Jamil bringing his son. She did not want to spoil her chances. So she accepted without further question. When Jamil had left she unpacked the food he had brought her and put it away in the 'fridge and the cupboards, then thought about her meal for the day. Jamil had been generous and her mood lightened. After making herself a dish of pasta spiced with a ready made sauce and topped with cheese, she was content to curl up on the sofa and flick through the tv channels until she found something she could watch. Still weary from the long journey into the country and a restless night, it was not long before she slipped into a comfortable sleep.

******

Later in the day Jamil absented himself from his office on the pretext of following up a lead. He took the tube to the station nearest to the lock-up, collected his car and drove home. Katya was cleaning the sitting room with Hasan laid on a blanket on the floor and Jamil's unexpected arrival surprised her. The baby, content and gurgling and stretching for the mirror on his play gym, screeched excitedly when Jamil entered the room and held out his arms to his father.

"Get his coat," Jamil instructed Katya. "I'm taking him out."

A sudden disquiet seized her but she covered her feelings as

26

best she could.

"Where? Where are you going?"

"Just out," Jamil snapped. "Maybe to the park. Maybe shopping. Just do it."

"I have taken him to the park already. Like you told me," Katya ventured carefully.

"Don't question me, woman. Just fetch his coat."

Jamil's expression was one of impatience.

"You'll need his pushchair – for the park?" suggested Katya.

"Of course. I will take it," and he settled Hasan into his car seat, strapped the car seat into the car and placed the pushchair in the boot.

"How long will you be?" Katya ventured. "He will need feeding soon."

"We will not be too long," Jamil replied, smiling to his son. "Just a little outing with your Baba, heh, Hasan?"

Katya watched them drive away. She had done as she was told but her heart was heavy. Jamil had never taken Hasan out before. Where were they going? And in the back of her mind, the fear hovered that Jamil may not bring Hasan back. But why should he do that? And where could he possibly take him? To this woman, maybe? Setting up another home to rob her of her son. She challenged herself. He could not take Hasan away without all his things. She was being paranoid, ridiculous. Why did she have this feeling of unease, a suspicion that was without foundation? She dismissed the notion and set about her chores once more.

******

The doors of the lift opened with a soft hiss and Jamil strode to the door of the apartment on the second floor, fumbling in his pocket for his key. Mina heard the key in the lock. Waking from her sleep she had cleaned the apartment with cleaning materials found in the kitchen cupboard and, pleasing to Jamil, the whole place smelled fresh and inviting. The afternoon sun streaming in through the windows on the river side had warmed the air and the tv was on a radio channel, so that music filled the apartment bringing it to life. When Jamil appeared in the doorway holding his son, Mina reacted with spontaneous joy.

"Oh, beautiful," she cried. "He is beautiful. What his name?"

"Hasan," Jamil replied. "His name is Hasan," and he sat on the sofa with Hasan on his knee. Mina knelt in front of the smiling infant and spoke to him gently.

"Hello, beautiful boy," she crooned. "And smiley. So smiley. Does he always?"

"Yes, he is a very happy baby," Jamil told her. "And he likes you. I can see."

Mina asked the question that had been on her mind.

"Where his mother?"

Jamil's face darkened and he paused, choosing his words with care.

"She is gone," he answered. "Left."

Mina exclaimed in disbelief.

"Oh, left this beautiful boy? Oh, how? Left this boy?"

"Yes," said Jamil abruptly. "No more questions."

Mina accepted, taking his abrupt tone as a sign of a painful experience, of an uncaring mother who had left them both. She said no more.

Jamil stayed for half an hour. He outlined to Mina her duties and her pay. She would be fed and housed in return for her care of Hasan and would receive a small allowance each month for herself. She was promised each Sunday for herself to do as she wished though in reality Jamil had little intention of allowing her such a luxury. As he prepared to leave, Mina asked again for a key.

"I will get one made for you," Jamil promised. "As soon as I can."

He left and took his son home, calling on the way at his usual petrol station where he bought a fluffy rabbit he had seen last time he had stopped for petrol. It was important, he had decided, that he lull Katya into a false sense of security, maybe let her think things were improving between them, that he was embracing his role and their family life. And while he drew the line at acts of affection between himself and his wife, indulging Hasan was no chore.

******

Katya gave a sigh of relief as she saw Jamil's car turn back into the driveway.

"See. You are just paranoid," she reassured herself. "He is back safe and sound."

Jamil carried the car seat back inside the house and placed it in the hallway. Hasan was sucking vigorously on the ear of the rabbit.

"Oh, you bought him a toy," exclaimed Katya, attempting to create a warmth between them. "And he loves it."

"Yes," Jamil replied. "I will be back later," he told her.

"Will you be home for supper?"

"Maybe. It depends on what is happening."

She made to kiss Jamil as he left but he brushed her aside as casually as he could.

******

Several hours later, when Jamil arrived back at his office, Len was mulling over the statement made by the driver of the lorry, a statement he considered vague with no real detail, just an unsubstantiated allegation.

"Did you get the manifest from the ferry company?" he asked.

"I have a copy. Just fetched it," Jamil replied, waving the large brown envelope he held in his hand.

"I want every vehicle on that manifest checked. Get onto the DVLA database and find out the owner of every vehicle that came over on that ferry. Make sure you do it yourself."

"Yes, sir."

Jamil turned to leave Len's office, then paused and turned back to face Len again, who gave him an enquiring look.

"Sir, it's about this possible insider information," he ventured. "I've been thinking about the team."

"Go on."

Well, there's just one person I have doubts about."

"Who is?"

"Jacob. Jacob Adama."

Len sat back in his seat, taking notice now.

"Jacob? Why Jacob? What's your reason for suspecting him?"

Jamil moved back towards the desk, leaning casually on the chair before it.

"I've noticed that he's out of the office for much longer than is necessary sometimes. When I ask him why he's been so long there's only a vague excuse; you know, traffic, disruption on the underground – that sort of thing."

"Is that all?"

"Well, he looks sort of shifty when he's saying it. And then there's his personal life. Jacob's single but he never talks about what he does outside of work. Never mentions friends or hobbies. If you ask him 'what are you doing at the weekend, Jacob?, he's sort of …. how do you say?"

"Secretive," Len suggested.

"Yes. Secretive. The other guys, they talk all the time about their wives and families, what they will be doing. You know, in the office, when they're down the 'pub after work. But not Jacob."

"Nothing else?"

"Not as yet, sir."

"It's a bit flimsy, Jamil. I'd need something a bit more concrete than that to suspect one of our own."

"I understand that, sir. It's just that I don't see anyone else as a possibility. As far as I can see, none of the others are in the least suspect."

"Well, I'll give it some thought. For the time being just

keep a diary of his movements. And best keep his involvement in cases to a minimum for now."

"Yes, sir."

Jamil turned and left with satisfaction. He knew Jacob's secret, his need for money. His companion was approving.

"Well done, Jamil. The seed has been sown; now it's up to you to follow it through."

It was early evening by the time he had finished working on the manifest and Len had already left. The office was now empty. He scanned the manifest onto his computer, deleted the details of the lorry that had been used to bring in the girls, then printed off a fresh copy. He spent more time writing on the newly edited manifest all the details he had garnered from the DVLA as though from his original enquiries with the odd crossing out or scribbled comment to add authenticity. When he had finished, he sat back and looked at the document, satisfied that it would pass inspection. By now it was well into the evening. About to head for the shredder in the post room to destroy the original copy, he was interrupted by the sound of an opening door. With a sharp intake of breath, he quickly stuffed the genuine document under a sheaf of papers in the bottom drawer of his desk as footsteps approached.

"Oh, it's you, Mr Hussein. I saw the light under the door and just came to check. I thought everyone had left. Sorry to disturb you."

It was Matt, the security guard, doing his rounds.

"No problem," Jamil replied. "I'm just leaving. Just had a job to finish, you know how it is?" and in a hurry he stood up and put on his jacket, placing the amended manifest in the top drawer of his desk which he locked with a key. He put the key in the breast pocket of his jacket and left the office with a cheery wave to Matt.

"Goodnight, Matt."

"Goodnight Mr Hussein."

Out in the cool air, Jamil let out a sigh, making a mental note to destroy the original manifest at his earliest opportunity. He wondered if he should have left it in the office at all. Why hadn't he brought his briefcase? But it was too late now to change things. There was no way he could return. It would have to do and in any case, as far as he knew he was the only one with a key to his desk. Having reassured himself, he made his way to an appointment with Sadie. The girl he had asked for would be waiting. He turned his mind to more pleasant thoughts and went on his way.

As Sadie had promised, the girl was waiting, already installed in the Green Room. As Jamil entered, she rose with trepidation and shrank back as he moved towards her. Her youthful figure was silhouetted in the light from the neons outside the window. Jamil felt himself harden at the thought of taking her. As he approached he saw her body tense and a whisper escaped from her lips.

"No. Please. No."

"Relax," he told her. "There is nothing to be afraid of. What is your name?"

"Sofiya," she told him.

"Well, Sofiya, come – join me in a drink."

"I wish leave," she told him.

"You will leave when I say," he told her, fixing her eyes with his own.

Her dark eyes, already large, widened further. The drink and the drugs took effect quickly and he took her once, then slept and on waking took her again. The blood on the sheets confirmed his expectation. She had been a virgin. It gave him satisfaction to know that he had been the first, strengthened his notion of power over her. So he left her in the early hours of morning with words of menace.

"Welcome to England and your new career."

Sofiya's story

Her arrival in the country with her sister was a time Sofiya would never forget. The journey had been tedious and uncomfortable, jolted and thrown about in the back of the lorry with every bump and curve in the road. The lorry smelled of damp cardboard from the boxes stacked precariously around them and it was dark and stuffy, like a poorly ventilated cell. Stepping out into the brightness at the end of the journey had been a relief if not entirely satisfying. It looked like some sort of warehouse, not a street in the city as they had expected. But then they were illegal with no realistic idea of what to expect. There was no itinerary for this mystery tour.

A group of people awaited their arrival, two women and man. After a brief stop for water and a sandwich, they were bundled into yet more transport for another journey. Only by then, he had arrived; this other man who would bring her such pain and who shamed her. She would shiver at the remembrance of him for many years to come.

Arriving on a wide street of smart buildings, she was ushered through a door, only realising too late and in panic that her sister was not behind her; only another girl who'd been one of their group. Inside the building the door clicked shut behind them as her sister was driven away. Her Ana? Where was she? She babbled the question to the young woman but the only response was a gruff instruction to move on.

"But I need know. Where my sister?"

"You'll have to ask Sadie in the morning. Now go."

With the door to the street closed and locked behind them, it was now too late; there was nothing she could do. For now, her Ana was gone. Showered and distressed but exhausted from the journey, she slept until the morning, hoping that this Sadie would give her the answer she implored.

The next day she waited patiently but it was not until the evening that the woman Sadie appeared. There was no answer to Sofiya's question, only "you'll see – later. Now you come with me. People are waiting to meet you."

Sadie drove her to another part of the city, a confused stranger in the teeming hustle and bustle of the night-time trade. Then another building, an old place that looked like a nightclub with a flashing neon sign emblazoned above the doorway. The woman Sadie took her to what she called The Green Room, a lavishly furnished softly-lit boudoir that made its purpose crystal clear. The shock of her situation and what she was now presented with rendered Sofiya almost numb.

"You change – into these," the woman instructed, taking from a drawer a set of lewd underwear and negligee. "And don't be long. Someone is waiting."

Perched on a chair by the satin-dressed bed, Sofiya twiddled nervously with the scanty clothing that Sadie had instructed her to wear. It clung transparent to her body and her dark glossy hair hung in ringlets around her slender neck. The clothes made her feel like a whore and she knew what was coming but not how to prevent it. When the man entered she rose with trepidation, shrinking back as he moved towards her. It was him, the man from the warehouse. Behind her the light from the host of neon signs that were Soho glowed outside the window, silhouetting her body and highlighting the slim youthfulness of her figure. As he approached her, she shrank back further with apprehension until she found herself pressed against the wall.

"Relax," he told her. "There is nothing to be afraid of. What is your name?"

"Sofiya,," she told him.

Well, Sofiya, come – join me in a drink."

"I want leave," she told him.

"You will leave when I say," he told her, fixing her eyes with his own.

Her dark eyes, already large, widened further.

"I was promised," she began. "Good work. Not this."

"Well, promises are sometimes broken," he answered. "But you are here, in England, where you wanted to be. You can have a good life, just as long as you do as you are told. Now drink," and he handed her a glass of sparkling wine laced with

34

rohipnol. In ignorance she sipped it reluctantly, thinking to play for time, but the drug and the alcohol needed little time to take effect. When he pulled her onto the bed beside him, she could offer nothing in the way of resistance. He enjoyed her supple young body, then slept until he was ready to take her again. He left her in the early hours of morning with the words 'welcome to England and your new career'.

Alone once the door had closed behind him, Sofiya turned onto her side, pulling the bedclothes around her, and, curling into the foetal position, she wept. And in her distress, she called out for Ana, fearful of what fate had befallen her loved younger sister. "I'm sorry, Ana. I'm so sorry."

Chapter Four

Friday 12th September

Hearing Jamil's key turn in the lock, Katya lay silently in the early morning darkness of the bedroom. She heard him go first to the nursery, then on to the bathroom, heard the cascade of water in the shower until several minutes later it ceased. She heard his soft tread as he headed for the bedroom, caught his reflection in the mirror as he entered the room, his lower body wrapped in a towel. Katya did not move, pretending she was still sleeping. She could hear his movements, the rustle of fabric as he put on the fresh clothes, a clean shirt, his business suit, she felt his eyes on her as he dressed. She stirred and pretended to open her eyes for the first time, turning to face him. He was sitting at the foot of the bed putting on his socks. She called his name and reached out her arm, touched his hand in a tender gesture but he raised from the bed and started to leave, at first hesitating, but then shaking her away.

"I will be back at lunchtime," he told her. "I will take Hasan to the park. Make sure he is ready." Then he was gone.

Katya sighed despondently.

"I am stupid to hope things will change," she told herself. "So stupid."

******

Outside Jamil paused at his car and sighed.

It's a pity," he thought. "I liked her once. We had fun. But now she's become a bore. A weight around my neck; a clinging wife like a vine choking my life. I don't need that. And I can't trust her to do as I say. Like all the women in my life, I can't trust her to be on my side. She is only out for herself. She has to go but without my son, my Hasan. And without my money."

******

Journey into Darkness

Katya's story

It was surely usual for a man or woman of the free world to have some control of their life, she thought; to make their own choices to fulfil their desired destiny, like the river outside her village in Turkey, forging its own path through sand and rock to make its course from the mountain down to the sea. Only fate or God's intervention should change their course, like that same river diverting its path around a granite hilltop heaved up in the course of creation. So why was her life so beyond her control? She pondered the state of her existence. She stretched her forefinger towards the hand of her baby son reclining in his baby seat, stroking the soft skin of his plump little fingers. He clasped her finger, curling his own around it in a tight grip and gurgled with joy. It was because of Hasan, it seemed to her. Hasan had been the intervention and was pivotal to the current state of affairs.

She loved her son, more than anything or anyone in the world. She had thought they would be such a happy family, her and Jamil and their child. But it had not worked out that way. They *had* been happy, she and Jamil – or so she had thought. And the event of her pregnancy at first had added joy. But then things had changed; subtle creeping changes that left their beginning unidentifiable and prevention beyond her control. And she was at a loss to understand why. Her life had become a mystery to her.

Sitting at the kitchen table sipping a cup of strong coffee Katya nursed a bruised and swollen face. It was not the first; merely the latest in a series. Before her on the table lay her purse and a bundle of receipts. She always collected them on her shopping trips to prove to Jamil she had spent her allowance on necessities. He was frugal with his money, an inquisition accompanying any suggestion that she needed more. Amongst the receipts she espied the corner of a crumpled photograph that she always carried with her. She pulled it from the pile and returned the smile on the happy faces of her long deceased parents looking up at her. They had died together on one terrible day many years before. The words of her grandmother, now also gone, spoken on the day of their funeral came back to her.

"Remember how dearly they loved you. Remember the love you shared. Hold onto that love for all your life, Katya. It will sustain you through the dark hours. We all have dark hours in our lives. You have yours now; I dare say you will have more. Hold onto that love to comfort you."

And she had done. Katya pressed the photograph to her breast and felt the love swell within. She held onto it tightly.

When she and Jamil had met, she had been working as an interpreter for an agency that had sent her to the Border Agency. An immigrant of several years standing, with a talent for languages, she had built herself a successful career. Happy with her life and in the country, she was in the process of applying for UK Citizenship. And then one red letter day, or so she had thought at the time, she had met Jamil.

Her task had been to interpret at the interview of a Russian suspected of trafficking. Jamil was the interviewing officer, also a long term immigrant who had built himself a comfortable career and lifestyle. The attraction between the two had been immediate. Katya was pretty. She was kind and loving, had been bubbly and confident then. She had been successful, with all the attributes that appealed to Jamil who, in his arrogance, considered himself a catch for any woman. He had charmed and cajoled her, wined and dined her, showered her with flowers and seemingly laid his heart at her feet. She could not know that to him she was simply the acceptable accessory, but most of all the wife he needed to give him the son he craved. Their relationship had progressed at a pace, passionate and intense and he had not so much as proposed to her as informed her that they would be married, a realisation that had only come to her later.

Once married, he had wanted her to give up her own employment, distracting her in one way or another so that increasingly she turned down assignments from the agency, unmindful of what was really happening, until the offers of work had ceased altogether.

"You do not need to work," he insisted. "You are my wife. That is enough."

"But I like to work. I like meeting people. Being involved. It is good – yes? And I earn money."

"I said no. You are a married woman now. Your place is at home. Having children."

"But not yet, surely, darling. We have only been married a short while. Perhaps in a year or so?"

Jamil's annoyance had been obvious, a potential for violence Katya had not seen before detectable in his demeanour. She had held her tongue.

Dependent on him for even her basic needs, she began to feel isolated and vulnerable, increasingly unable to resist his demands. Even so, all had remained reasonable between them until she had become pregnant with Hasan. At first Jamil had greeted the news with pride, referring to the baby as 'his son' despite her reminders that it could indeed be a girl. But as her belly began to swell, Jamil became increasingly cold towards her, spending long hours away from the house, sometimes even days, which he blamed of course on the irregular hours of his work. But she knew otherwise. She could smell the women on him when he came home, a sickening smell that told her the unique bond between them was broken. At first she had challenged him.

"You are late again, my darling. So busy?"

"Are you complaining? It is my job. It keeps a roof over your head and food on the table."

Then the violence had began, mild at first, a slap, a grip on her arm that left it bruised. Out of concern for her unborn child, again she held her tongue, comforting herself with the bond between herself and her baby. She would talk to her child, smiling and crooning, caressing her swollen belly in the increasing hours of solitude. The loneliness was hard to bear. She began to suspect, too, that Jamil was not the servant of the country she had thought him to be. The wads of money she would sometimes glimpse in his possession warned her that he had other activities far more lucrative than the salary she imagined he received. His modest car had been replaced with a more prestigious model, the suits more expensive, the Rolex watch flamboyant, none of which were displayed during his working hours and with no reference or explanation to her. To his colleagues at the Border Agency he presented his usual self displaying nothing ostentatious, arriving at work in the capital by public transport or collected by a colleague when on surveillance, his working clothes modest, the Rolex secreted away at home in a drawer. She asked no questions, fearful of the response any curiosity might bring. In the rose-tinted haze of her passion, Katya had seen the man Jamil had wanted her to see and only now, too late, were the veils of the illusion falling from her eyes. Still she struggled against acceptance of reality, of the man he truly was and her status in his life, excusing the bouts of anger, the coldness, as lapses brought about by pressures in his work and her own faults and lack of understanding.

When Hasan had been born, Jamil had been noticeably moved. He held his newborn in his arms and kissed the soft downy hair and forehead.

"My beautiful son," he crooned. "My beautiful Hasan."
He had named the baby without reference to or consideration of the mother but overlooking the exclusion, she still hoped the man she believed him to be would return.

"We are a family now, Jamil. The three of us, a happy family." Her hopes had been short lived. Indeed now Jamil's attitude towards her was not just cold but became one of cruelty. He imposed strict rules with regard to the baby. When he was at home, Hasan would be with him constantly, her presence required only when the baby needed a change of nappy or some other basic attention.

"Get on with your job," her would tell her. "I have shirts that need ironing. Do you want me seen at work looking like a tramp?"

He insisted she cease breast feeding when Hasan was only weeks old so that he could feed him with a bottle, talking and stroking the baby's head as he held him close to his body, reinforcing the bond between them to her exclusion. Their relationship became one of master to a servant, her function to care for the needs of himself and his child.

In Jamil's absence, she tried secretly to breast feed Hasan, cherishing the bond between them, but it was not to be. Struggling against depression, the stress and hurt inhibited her ability to lactate. Still she would hold the baby to her empty naked breasts just for the joy of his skin against her own and talk to her son like any loving mother.

"My best boy," she called him. "My Hasan."

Hasan was her saving grace.

He was now 5 months old and it tortured her each time Jamil returned to see the strengthening bond between father and son to her exclusion. It cut deep, like a knife plunging into her heart. She feared the coldness the separation would bring as Jamil again dismissed her from their company. Towards her there was no affection, no love-making, not so much as a kiss. She wondered constantly how her life had come to this, to such darkness from the bright beginnings and how she could recover the way things had once been. Deep down she knew the answer. It was all about Jamil. Something within his psyche was wrong, his self-obsession and his obsession with his son.

Jamil was a tortured man, she knew that too. There were the nightmares that woke him sweating and shaking and tainted his

41

humour for days. She had tried to gently probe but he would tell her nothing. There must be something in his past that troubled him and whatever it was, she believed it to be real and it was bad. Was it something he had done or something he had suffered? She did not know.

Her only lifeline was Helen, the Health Visitor who had visited after Hasan's birth and who she dared to see from time to time at the Mother and Baby Centre, an outing Jamil allowed for the welfare of his son. Helen questioned her with concern, the dark shadows around the eyes, the change in demeanour. Used to seeing new and young mothers suffering the effects of sleep deprivation with a new and demanding infant to care for, Helen clearly suspected that this was different so Katya tried to conceal it or explain away the tell tale signs of abuse. There was occasional discolouration of the skin, old bruising that became visible when Helen made an excuse to pry.

"Can you roll up your sleeve, please, Katya? Baby's fine so I just need to check you over. Let's take your blood pressure; make sure there's no problem there."

Or a tell-tale sign would be impossible to conceal, the cut of a lip or a flinch of discomfort when touched. Once or twice Helen had pressed her about the bruising but there were always excuses, a fall or a bump against a door that was to blame. But deep down Katya knew that Helen was not convinced,.

"You are hurt again, Katya? Another bruise?"

Oh, I am so clumsy, Helen. Always falling or bumping," and she would feign an apologetic smile.

"We'd better check your blood, Katya. Just to make sure you are not anaemic or anything else that may be making you unwell. Do you feel dizzy or faint at all?"

Shaking her head she would dismiss any such suggestion.

"I am just clumsy," she insisted. "Always falling."

Katya was grateful for Helen's visits – her only visitor, the closest she had to a friend - and it was on one such visit, when a bruised rib was too painful to make the journey to the surgery, that she finally admitted the truth.

"I don't know why he does it. We were so happy. Before.... " Her voice trailed off. Helen was indignant.

"It's about control, Katya. He wants to control you. To dominate you. But it's your life. You don't have to put up with it. There are places you can go. With Hasan. Safe places to stay and help to get your life sorted out."

Katya had paused, then began, "Where I come from .... ". She stopped. How could she tell Helen that where she came from it was not unusual for a man to beat his wife? Her pride would not let her admit what she knew Helen would regard with disdain. Katya waited for Helen's response. For a moment there was only silence but then it came, an urging once more that Katya take action before the situation became worse. But Katya would not be persuaded.

"Jamil would not allow it. His pride would not allow it, especially me taking Hasan. He would find us. Be even more angry. Violent. I would be very afraid. No. I have to stay - at least until Hasan is older. Then I will stand up for myself; for what I want, too."

Alone after Helen's visit, Katya settled Hasan in his cot and went to the bedroom to change out of her outdoor clothing. Catching sight of herself in the mirror, she stripped to her underwear and studied her body. Jamil had not touched her since Hasan was born other than to hit her. She knew he indulged his sexual needs elsewhere. Why, she wondered, did he now find her so repulsive? She ran her fingers across her belly, her stomach almost as flat now as before her pregnancy, her breasts still firm and milk free and her nipples no longer sore since she had ceased to feed Hasan. Despite the tiredness a new born infant imposed, she did her best to always look nice when Jamil came home, though it was hard to do since his movements were so unpredictable. If she could just re-ignite the passion they had previously enjoyed, maybe they could recover the warmth of their relationship and the violence would end. But how? She had considered the candlelit supper, the seductive scene, but again difficult when she was never sure when he would be home. She could cook him one of his favourite meals, maybe *mumta*; he loved mumta. But when? And how? She never drank alcohol; her religion forbade it and she disliked the smell of it on Jamil's breath. But it would be a price worth paying to regain their relationship so she had bought his favourite beer and set it in the 'fridge. It made no difference, he never stayed at home to drink.

Helen's words rang in her head. She considered the option of leaving but she was alone in the world now, no family in Turkey to support her if she left the country with Hasan and no chance of escaping Jamil if she did not. Despite their longing, her parents had not been blessed with more children leaving Katya an only child, no siblings to confide in or depend on. Her father had been wounded when she was only 9 years old, caught by enemy fire along with thousands of his compatriots in Northern Iraq in an offensive against the Kurds. On his return a wounded civilian, her Mother had cared for her husband tenderly and their relationship had endured as one of deep love and mutual respect, unlike others in their village where wives were afforded little affection or value. It was the benchmark set for Katya in a relationship of her own, a benchmark of which her marriage was falling so far short.

In 1999 disaster had struck once more.   With the exception of herself, then a teenager and her widowed grandmother, pulled from the rubble dazed and dirty but gratefully physically unhurt, the remainder of the family were amongst the 17,000 residents killed by the massive earthquake that shook the northern country. From its epicentre in Izmit the shock-waves had spread as far as Istanbul, 50 miles away, destroying buildings and infrastructure in their path. The stress of the trauma had stayed with Katya for several years, disturbing her sleep with nightmares of those early morning hours when they had been thrown from their beds. She had salvaged only one thing from the wreckage, her precious Pippa doll bought for a birthday by her parents. It was broken and twisted, the clothes filthy, the long silky blonde hair dust-laden and an eye damaged.

"Like me," she thought. "I am damaged and broken too." But she had cleaned her Pippa, brushed the hair until the debris was all removed, and she had kept it with her in her bedroom all her life since until Jamil had thrown it into the bin,. Once he had left for work, she had retrieved it and hidden Pippa in the bottom of one of her drawers.

Her confidence and security had been destroyed by the earthquake and replaced with fear and uncertainty. In later years, recovering a degree of empowerment, Katya had travelled to England as an immigrant, to use the English she had studied hard at school to provide for her ageing grandmother. Her grandma, her *Ebe*, had spoken as they sat on two white plastic chairs outside their modest home in the dust patch that served as a garden.

"You must make a life for yourself, Katya. I will not be here for ever. Go build a good life. Find a good man. You are clever. You are beautiful inside and out, too good for the louts in these parts," and she had spat her disdain into the dust beside her.

"But you, *Ebe*? How can I leave you?"

"I will be fine just as long as I know you are well and happy. Old Boy next door will keep an eye on me."

Their parting had been emotional but her grandmother had encouraged her on. When she had proudly taken Jamil to visit her *Ebe*, by then terminally ill with cancer, the response had surprised and dismayed her.

"Don't marry him, Katya. He is not good for you."

"*Ebe*, why do you say such a thing? I love him and he loves me."

"He has cold eyes, Katya. Unkind eyes. His mouth smiles but not his eyes. Please Katya. Listen to your grandmother."

When the old lady had succumbed to the cancer, Katya had pondered those words but Jamil's charm and attentiveness had persuaded her that the old lady had been wrong, that her grandmother had become a possessive and lonely old lady trying to hang on to her much loved child. As time had passed, the memory of her grandmother's warning had echoed in Katya's mind until at this moment her words returned along with those of Helen. Should she leave Jamil, now, before things became worse and he really hurt her? But where to go? How to survive? Alone and without a home or money. And the fear of what Jamil would do if she took Hasan from him kept her rooted to the spot. So here she must remain. This was her choice, but not one made freely. The day would come, she promised herself; a day when she would take back control of her life. She would not accept this for ever.

Dismissing her thoughts, she drew her dressing gown around her and went to the nursery. Kneeling beside her sleeping son she watched the gentle rise and fall of his breathing.
"My boy," she whispered. "My beautiful boy."
In her darkest nightmare, she would not have foreseen the events about to overtake her.

******

In the afternoon Jamil took Hasan once more to see Mina.
"When will he come? To stay," she asked.
"When we have everything ready, Mina," Jamil assured her.
"Today I will buy the things for his room. Maybe by the weekend we will be ready."
"Where he live now?"
"With his Auntie but she cannot keep him there. She already has her own children. So it will happen soon."
As he made to leave, Mina asked again.
"The key?"
"Oh, Mina. I'm so sorry. I forgot to do it. I have been so busy. I will bring it soon, I promise."
Mina did not reply. But she was bored with being indoors, like

a prisoner; nothing to do each day but watch tv and eat. Jamil had brought more food and drink so she was not hungry. But she was alone. And the loneliness was hard to bear.

"When Hasan comes," she told herself," it will be better. It will be soon".

Returned home once more, Jamil left Hasan with his mother. He drove to the lock-up to draw a wad of cash from a safe against the back wall , then on to a branch of Mothercare outside of town. He had looked around Hasan's nursery at home and taken note of his needs, of the formula and nappies that Katya bought him. He chose a cot and bedding, a bath and changing mat and towels, a play gym, some toys and a set of dishes. He had seen that Katya used a special bag to carry everything when she took Hasan out so he bought another. Lastly he stopped at a supermarket and bought the formula and nappies. As he moved towards the checkout he walked down the baby aisle, thinking as he went. Bath lotion, creams and shampoo; yes, he would need those too. Congratulating himself on his organisation, he paid for his goods and made his way back to the Mercedes. At the apartment in Docklands, he left it all with Mina.

"Yes, I will find places for everything," she told him. "But the cot. How I do it?"

"I will put it together," he told her. "When I come back."

"And Hasan. When?"

"Maybe tomorrow, maybe the next day. The weekend when I am not working."

Jamil considered in his mind. Today is Friday. It is my weekend off so this would be a good time to do it. Yes. I have the drugs for Katya. I've found a place to take her, the disused warehouse along the river, going out to sea. No-one will hear her there. No-one will find her until she is taken. Yes, this is the weekend. All is prepared. He had given Mina a 'phone in which the only number was his own.

"You do not call me unless it is urgent," he told her. "My work

– I cannot be interrupted, except if it is urgent. Do you understand?"

She nodded.

The number of the phone he gave her he had put into his pay-as-you-go phone, both phones untraceable to inquisitive eyes. "I will call you," he told her. "And let you know when I am coming."

He left to return to his office, tension rising within him. His plan was already under way.

******

The general hubbub of day to day business filled the office as he arrived back at his desk. Conscious that the original manifest from the ferry company was still in the bottom drawer, he waited for an opportunity to destroy it without further delay but his wish was to be short-lived. It was not long before Len's head appeared around his office door with a new instruction.

"Jamil, you're needed at Heathrow," he called. "Details here," and he waved a paper in Jamil's direction.

"Heathrow?" echoed Jamil. "Where's their usual officer?"

"One off sick and the other on holiday. We'll have to send someone. I want you to go and take the new trainee with you; what's his name?"

"Sean," Jamil offered.

"Yes, Sean. Take him and show him the ropes. And by the way, that other person we were discussing. I'm not convinced but I've put him on surveillance anyway. Carry on with the diary and keep me informed."

"Yes sir, of course."

Jamil took the paper from Len with an inner satisfaction. His companion was jubilant.

"Good work, Jamil. It is working. Time now to take the next step, phase two of your plan for Jacob. They will need evidence – motive. A smoking gun. It can only be money to make him look greedy, just after the money."

"No problem," Jamil thought. "I have money. It will be done."

He grabbed his jacket from the back of his chair, checked that his desk was locked, then headed for the door tapping Sean's shoulder on the way.

"You're to come with me," he called. "Come on. Now."

"Where to?" asked Sean, jumping enthusiastically to his feet and switching his computer into standby mode. He trailed behind Jamil as they made their way towards the exit.

The interview at Heathrow took longer than Jamil had hoped for; first the wait for the interviewing officer, then a discussion as to whether they needed an interpreter. Jamil became impatient.

"Well, surely we can begin. If we need an interpreter we will soon know. We can't hang around for ever, we have other things to deal with."

It was agreed. The young woman claimed to be visiting a friend for a holiday but her excessive luggage had revealed a laptop and the files stored that she had contacted various agencies for work.

"Only for holiday money," she insisted. "Not for always." Jamil did not believe her.

"Stupid woman," he thought. "What fool does she take me for?"

"You cannot work here on a visitor's visa," he told her. "Access to the country is denied."

And so it was done.

By the time he and Sean had returned to the office it was well into the evening but the office was still the scene of frantic activity on another case. Jamil swore under his breath, recognising that now was not the time to deal with the manifest. It would have to wait until Monday. On consideration he decided it would be best to go home, get a good night's sleep and set things in motion with Katya in the morning. All was in order. He went through his mental check list; the last consignment was concluded and Mina was in place; the manifest had been amended and replaced and Len had no suspicion of him, focused instead on Jacob. He was in control. Now he must buy the things he needed for the next stage.

Before returning home, he called at a DIY store, selecting the items he needed and paying in cash. Then hailing a cab, he went to the lock-up to make the car ready. Already in the boot was a new holdall bought especially. Putting on a pair of latex gloves, he opened the safe and counted out £5000. in used £20. notes. From his inner pocket, he took out two envelopes brought from Jacob's desk in the office. He placed the £5000. neatly inside one envelope, sealed it and put the envelope inside the holdall, He zipped and locked the holdall and placed it in the boot of the car together with a length of rope and a roll of wide tape. In the other envelope he put the £1000. in used £10. notes and this time deliberately carelessly tucked in the flap so the banknotes were visible at one corner. He stuffed this envelope into the inner pocket of his jacket. Confident that he had thought of everything, he locked the car securely and left the lock-up, padlocking the door securely behind him and secreting the key under a manual in the glove compartment. Excitement was rising within him. He felt in control of his life and his agenda. All was ready.

Journey into Darkness

Chapter Five

Saturday 13th September – am

The morning broke to a dismal, heavily laden sky. When Jamil rose, the smell of freshly perked coffee wafted to greet him as he went down the stairs. Katya was already dressed and downstairs. She was making a bottle for Hasan, also washed and dressed and sitting in his baby chair. At the sight of his father, he beamed his usual welcome.

"Morning, darling. You are early. I thought you would sleep late on your weekend off."

Jamil grunted a response.

"I have things to do. In the office maybe."

He approached his objective with care. Taking the pot of coffee he placed it on the table with two cups and saucers.

"Good morning, Hasan," he crooned. "And how is my son this morning."

He kissed Hasan on his cheeks and ruffled his hair gently.

"I will feed him," he told Katya. "Here – I have poured you coffee."

His demeanour was amicable, a change from the normally sullen tone in which he would address her. Katya shook the baby bottle and tested the temperature of the milk on the back of her hand.

"It is ready," she told him.

She placed the bottle on the table close to Hasan's chair and proceeded to seat herself beside him where Jamil had placed her cup of coffee. She sipped at her coffee slowly, biting back her protest.

"I want to feed him," she wanted to say but she held her tongue.

"Why has he poured me coffee?" she wondered. "Why is he being nice today? Yesterday the fluffy rabbit for Hasan, today he is pouring me coffee? Speaking to me like he used to."

Perhaps it was a thaw in the coldness of recent months.

Perhaps the bad times really were over. Perhaps at last they were to be the happy family she had longed for. But the seeds of mistrust had been sown now; bitter, tangled shoots had taken root in every corner of her mind. The trust - if not entirely gone - was extremely shaky. Before she could consider further, events moved on.

Sitting on a chair on the other side of Hasan, Jamil feigned a spill of milk on Hasan's bib.

"Oh, damn," he exclaimed. "His bib is soaked. Katya, fetch another from his room."

While Katya responded to his bidding, he took the rohipnol from his dressing gown pocket and dropped it into her coffee. By the time Katya returned, it had dissolved without a trace. Jamil watched Katya intently as she sipped the warm liquid, waiting for the rophipnol to take effect.

As Jamil fed Hasan his bottle, Katya slithered across the table in a drug-induced faint. Jamil reached across and brushed back her soft golden hair. It had spread like sunlight across the dark surface of the table and once again he recalled their early days, the touch of those tresses falling gently against his cheek as they embraced. He lifted her eyelids one by one but they fell back heavily when he let them go, covering the beautiful eyes he had once found so appealing.

"You have wonderful eyes," he had told her. "Clear. Deep. Like I could swim in the light from them. So beautiful. And your golden hair."

He recalled the moment but instantly brushed the memory aside.

"What is this Jamil? Are you weakening now?" his companion admonished him.

"No, no. It is time, believe me. She is still beautiful but a nuisance now. It is the right thing to do. It would be necessary sooner or later anyway. Better sooner than later, while Hasan is still small enough to forget his mother. No-one will come looking for her now the old woman is gone. And if anyone else asks, she has simply left us - me and Hasan."

The old woman had not liked him, he knew it; those sharp, beady eyes boring into him like they could plumb the very depths of his soul. He had turned away from them, not wanting her to see what was so easily concealed from Katya's gentle, trusting gaze.

"Everything is arranged," his companion reminded him. "Get on with it. It is not the first time. No-one suspected before. No-one will now."

He pulled himself up abruptly, checked Katya's eyes once more for any sign of consciousness but there was none. He worked quickly.

Strapping Hasan safely back into his car seat, he ran up the stairs two at a time to the bedroom and threw on a pair of joggers and a sweatshirt. Then back down stairs again, he put on his trainers, grabbed his car keys and took Hasan, drowsy from the effect of a full stomach, out to the car, settling him with his fluffy rabbit. He looked up and down the street beyond the small forecourt and front garden, finding the usual quiet of an early Saturday morning. He had backed the car onto the forecourt the previous evening with the boot, which he now opened, being closest to the house. The holdall full of cash retrieved from the lock-up the previous evening remained secreted in the corner. Collecting the rope and the tape from the boot, he returned to see to Katya. After checking yet again that she remained unconscious, he lay her on the floor, cutting the rope into lengths to tie her hands behind her back and to bind her feet together. He hesitated at the tape which he decided right now was not necessary. She was incapable of calling to anyone. He carried her over his shoulder to the front door and in the absence of any other person within sight, placed her carefully into the boot of the car and closed it tight. So far so good.

The drive to the old warehouse took little time and being in a state of dereliction he again found it deserted. Driving the car through the once-padlocked doors into its interior, he made a mental note that once his job was done, he must replace the chain and padlock he had cut through, leaving the key in the appointed place. He opened the boot of the car, lifted out the still-unconscious Katya and carried her to the farthest corner of the darkened building. He laid her against the cold brick wall and taped her mouth tightly and fetched the holdall from the boot of the car which he laid beside her. He looked once more at her unconscious body. She would not wake for some time and by then the deed would be done. Satisfied that all was secure, he backed out of the warehouse and closed the doors. He took his pay-as-you-go phone from his pocket and keyed in a number. A voice answered the call.

"Allo."

"It is me. The package is ready for collection."

"In the agreed place?"

"Yes. The key for the padlock is under a stone by the door."

"And the collection fee?"

"In a bag with the package."

"I will see to it today."

"You will let me know when it has been despatched."

"Yes."

"Good. I need to know when it is done."

Jamil killed the call, satisfied with the response.

His next task was to take Hasan to Mina. He would leave him with her for a while for them to become acquainted but decided he would keep him at home at night. Mina was delighted when they arrived and Jamil told her he was leaving Hasan with her. Hasan had awoken and gurgled contentedly in his seat.

"I will fetch him later. He will stay with me at night – at the weekends. We must take things one step at a time."

"Can I take him out?" asked Mina. "The key?"

"Oh, Mina, I will get one today. I am sorry," and he feigned an apologetic smile. "And I have forgotten his pushchair. You stay with him here today."

Disappointed but accepting, Mina said no more. She lifted Hasan from his car seat and played tickling his chin with his rabbit. Confident his son would be in good hands, Jamil took his leave.

Blotting out the enormity of his actions, Jamil called Sadie from his car and asked once more to arrange for Sofiya. "Hmm, having a little bother there, I'm afraid," Sadie told him. "She really isn't ready, Jamil. Can you settle for Ebony this time?"
Jamil was not pleased.
"Why? What's the problem?" he asked sharply.
"Well, Sapphire called me yesterday. It seems that one of the girls here is her sister. Anastasiya. Sofiya's screaming and yelling that she wants to see Anastasiya. She became quite aggressive towards Sapphire. We're having to keep her locked in her room for the moment, until she calms down a little. Trouble is, we're having the same problem here with the sister. We may have to move them together. I don't like to let these girls dictate but I don't want the disruption either. Not good for the clients. I don't want it ending in losing either of them. I've invested too much. I'll let you know but in the meantime ...."
"Well, that is for you to deal with, Sadie. That is your problem," he interrupted. "OK, I will take Ebony this time. I will come tomorrow, about this time. But I'll have the other girl as soon as she is ready."
"It will happen," Sadie assured him. "Just as soon as we've tamed her a little."
"But not too much," Jamil answered with a grin in his voice. "Not too tame, heh?"
Sadie ignored his comment, humouring Jamil in the interest of business and made the arrangement for Ebony. But she didn't like violence with the girls. It was bad for business ,her business, disrupting if the clients heard and saw the bruising. She said nothing.

Jamil ended the call and thought about what Sadie had told

him. He liked the girls to be a little feisty. This new one had
not yet met with expectation, the soporific effect of the drug
had impeded the opportunity for fun. Next time would be
different, he hoped. Next time there would be more of a
challenge. And if she resisted, so much the better for the sport.
In the end, she would do as she was told.

******

The house appeared silent and deserted as Helen stood at the
door. She was concerned. Katya had not come to see her at the
clinic as she had asked and she was worried about her welfare.
"If I just call at the house as a friend," she wondered. "Maybe
I could just keep an eye on her on a casual basis. If I went in
the morning – on Saturday. I could take some flowers."
She was grateful that the husband's car was not there, unsure of
how he would react to her appearance but convinced that she
really had to try. With no response to her knock and no sign or
sound of movement within, she peered through the letterbox, a
little nervous that Jamil could arrive at any moment. She could
see Hasan's pushchair folded in the hallway, his warm outdoor
suit and blanket placed on top ready for use. But still there was
no response. Stepping back from the door she pondered. What
should she do? She had no proof that anything was wrong –
just a gut feeling of anxiety that would not let her go. Leaving
the house perplexed she returned to her car and sat for a while,
hoping that Katya would appear. But in vain.
"I'll l talk to Martin. He's a policeman. He'll tell me what's
best to do."

'Hello, Coz. To what do I owe this unexpected pleasure?'
PC Martin Farrell addressed his cousin through the partition at
the station.
"Hi, Martin. I wondered if you could spare me a minute. If I
could have a word?"
"Hang on a jiffy. I'll come round."
Martin disappeared from behind the screen and reappeared

through a security door to the side of her.

"What's the problem?"

"It's one of my young mums. I can't get hold of her and I'm a bit worried something may have happened to her."

"Why would you think that? I mean, she could be with family, at friends, gone away, out on a shopping spree. Whatever. Why the concern?"

"Well, she has no family; not in this country anyway. And no friends I'm aware of. But she does have an abusive husband."

"Oh, right. I see. But I can't do anything just because you're concerned, Helen; you can understand that, can't you?"

"Yes, I know that, Martin; but I just thought you might be able to check – like hospitals, or something."

"Look, I'm really busy right now. Can I come and see you when I've finished my shift?"

"Of course. Will Jules be with you?"

"No, she's off on a hen do. I'm on my own for the weekend."

"Oh, well why don't I do supper then?"

"Now there's an offer I can't refuse. What time?"

"About seven suit you?"

"Seven it is. And then you can tell me all about this mum of yours."

******

At the other end of the 'phone, Ross McKinnon smiled with satisfaction as the call from Jamil had died. He keyed another number on the keypad. When he had seen the photo of Katya sent to him by Jamil it had seemed to him that a straightforward disposal of such an asset was a terrible waste. So with an alternative scenario in mind, he had made enquiries amongst his associates. It would be easy to place her with one of them and earn a second commission. He had contacts who ran premises where women were kept secure. Ultimately it was one such contact in the north who had made the best offer. Katya's photo had excited the man. She would be perfect to gratify himself and his son; and for his wife an unpaid domestic servant. He was wealthy. He lived in a semi-rural environment behind an electronically controlled fence and gates - not to mention the dogs - so security would not be an issue. Ross had considered it the perfect placement. Ross keyed in the number and the man, too, was pleased to receive a call.

"I'll deliver your goods this evening, if that suits."

"Certainly. All is ready. I look forward to your arrival."

Ross made himself a coffee. He lit a cigarette and relaxed back in his seat for a while content that he was about to earn himself another nice fat fee. Ross McKinnon ran the print company that had been started by his father, a bully of a man who had abused Ross's mother until she had killed herself in despair. It was 10-year old Ross who had returned from school one afternoon to find his mother unconscious in her bed in the flat above the print works and an empty tablet bottle on the floor beside. He had called an ambulance but his mother had never regained consciousness. Left at the mercy of his abusive father, Ross had withdrawn into his inner self and grown up socially and physically inept. When he left school with little academic achievement to recommend him for any career, he worked in the print firm with his father, reproducing by the hundred weight pornographic material imported from the continent for the local market. De-sensitized by the constant barrage of images, rather than indulging in sexual perversion, his interest in the opposite sex was nil. He simply viewed women as commercial trash.

When his father, by then a pensioner, had died from what Ross assumed to be a heart attack, it seemed to him that no-one else really needed to know.

"No-one likes him. No-one cares about him - Billy no-mates. Why pay for the cost of a funeral? I'll just tell people he's retired and gone to live in Spain," and he had laughed at the prospect of the deception. So under cover of darkness he had buried him in the small yard at the rear and relaid the flagstones

to cover his handiwork. He would smile to himself with
satisfaction whenever a reference was made in jest, on tv or by
an unsuspecting innocent, to 'the body under the patio'. Even
so, he rarely sat out there, an uncomfortable feeling when he
tried that a hand might reach up from the depths and draw him
downwards into the dark, cold earth. He lived his life indoors,
often on his computer in the basement, like a troglodyte with IT
skills.

When he was forced to leave the property, either for his
own needs or on business, it gave him pleasure to drive
his father's car abandoning the ancient and uncomfortable pick-
up that he had been taught to drive in and which he used to
deliver their merchandise, mostly under cover of darkness. For
the first time in his life, he found himself free to pursue his own
agenda - and he had done so with alacrity. He had no feelings
towards the people he trafficked, neither compassion nor
disdain. They were simply commodities, the subjects of
commercial transaction. Finishing his cigarette and his coffee,
he moved to the safe in the corner of the kitchen and tapped in
the combination, opening the door to reveal an interior stacked
with paper money. He took £100. for petrol and subsistence
and the photograph of Katya that had been emailed by Jamil.
Making the safe secure once more, he prepared to leave for his
journey feeling unconcerned by the task that lay ahead.

Ross's print shop was on the outskirts of Romford. He joined
the M25 and headed south towards Dartford, driving the Jaguar
steadily and comfortably within the speed limit to avoid
attracting unwanted attention. The banknotes were in his
wallet, the picture of Katya on the seat beside him, the petrol
gauge registered a full tank and the traffic was reasonably light.
He had lined the boot of the car with a new sheet bought
especially for the purpose which would be burned on
completion of the task. Even the weather was pleasing, the
earlier morning cloud now dispersed to permit a weak but
heart-warming sunshine. Relaxed against the softness of the

leather, he felt in control. The sudden change of pace ahead of him took him by surprise.

Travelling in the outside lane overtaking a van, the speedo on the mini was touching 75 miles an hour when the tyre burst. Its young and inexperienced driver swore in panic as the vehicle careered out of control. Swerving into the middle lane, it clipped the van and their bumpers tangled, carrying them both into the inside lane just ahead of Ross. Jerked out of his complacency, Ross attempted to avoid collision, braking hard, his foot slammed down on the pedal but it wasn't enough. All three vehicles tangled together and mounted the bank at the side of the motorway. Ross's car, being heavier than the other two, overturned and slid on its roof back down onto the carriageway where it was in collision yet again with a heavily-laden lorry carrying building bricks. The lorry driver braked but the weight of the lorry and its cargo bowled on, carrying Ross and his upturned vehicle along the inside lane until, finally, both vehicles came to a halt yards down the carriageway.

Vehicles pulled up on the hard shoulder behind them, their occupants leaping out to see what assistance they could offer. Mobile phones were ringing the emergency services, feet running, voices raised and shouting instruction from one to the other. The lorry driver leapt from his cab and with others attempted to help the occupants of each vehicle. Ross heard none of it. Ross was already dead, his neck snapped like a twig.

******

In the semi-darkness of the deserted warehouse, Katya had stirred. Her brain still fuzzy from the rohipnol, she lapsed in and out of consciousness, her mind playing tricks on her and the eyes she had always trusted trying to fool her, for all around her was unfamiliar, a strange sight, a place where she did not belong. It took time for the reality of her plight to register. At first she imagined herself back in Turkey, amongst the rubble of the earthquake where she and her grandmother had taken refuge under her grandmother's bed from the falling bricks and debris.

"Hold my hand, Katya; it will be over soon. Hold tight." But it had not been soon for the tremor was greater than anyone had expected and the aftershocks prolonged. She had heard the calling voices.

"We are coming. We are coming," and felt the rush of cool air as debris was cleared away.

She tried to move her hands behind her back but something was holding them preventing movement, some lump of concrete or piece of furniture that had her trapped. She tried to call but her mouth was not working. But as the mist in her brain cleared and reality took hold, she realised that her hands were tied behind her, her legs and feet bound at the ankles and her mouth taped. She fumbled through the confusion to disbelief, from disbelief to horror. This was not the earthquake, not a bad dream, a nightmare from which she would wake soon. It was real. How did this happen? Who had done this to her? Surely not Jamil? Not this. Even Jamil could surely not sink to this. Yes -Jamil. Who else? And where was she in this strange, unholy place? Where was her baby, her beautiful Hasan? The tears began to fall, the panic to rise. She sobbed and the tape stung tight against the skin of her lips. A scream rose in her throat.

"Hasan," her brain screamed. "Hasan."

She lay helpless in the dust until, still weak from the drugs and overwhelmed by shock and emotion, she sank back into sleep.

Chapter Six

Saturday, 13th September – pm

By the time Katya awoke for a second time, dusk was falling. At first she relived her initial confusion but reality came quicker this time. And this time, hot on its heels, came another realisation.

"If I want to see my Hasan again, I have to survive. I have to get out of here."

Straining her neck she raised her head to look around her. She tried to sit up but her strength failed her. Rolling onto her side she bent her knees up to her chin and tried to get up onto her knees, rocking her body to and fro until she was face down. Steadying her breathing she tried to sit up but her head fell forward and she hit her forehead with a bang on the hard stone of the floor. She stayed crouched on her knees for a moment, breathing heavily, then with one great effort heaved herself up onto her knees. Her head throbbed and she was tired from the effort but gratified that she had got this far. She rested back on her heels for several moments until, gathering every ounce of strength she could muster, with one great push she lifted herself onto her feet. Exhausted from the effort, she slouched against the wall and paused again to steady her breathing. Her mouth was dry as chaff, her stomach groaning with hunger. Her bladder was threatening to burst and she tried to control it but unable to cross her legs to hold back, she felt the heat of her urine saturating her jeans. She dropped her head, feeling her humiliation, a tear sliding down her cheek but she checked herself sharply.

"Keep calm, Katya," she counselled. "You must stay calm. You have to do this. Think of Hasan. Just think of your beautiful boy."

Once calmer and with her breathing restored to a steady rhythm, she studied the landscape around her. The state of dereliction told her that no-one would find her here, that somehow she must get out of this building to get help. She wondered whether Jamil would come back to kill her – or someone else that he had paid, a contract killer. Before now she would have thought that melodramatic, but no longer. At her feet lay a small holdall. It looked clean; brand new. Was it her clothes or was it money to pay for her disposal? Or had he intended just to leave her here to starve to death? Whatever the answer, there was no doubt in her mind now that he planned to be rid of her. Why had he not just divorced her? Why all this? It was Hasan. It had to be. She had always known it. The answer was Hasan. And she may not have long before he or someone returned to fulfil his intentions. She set to, exploring for a possible exit.

One jump at a time she made her way towards a window where cracks of dying daylight seeped through the gaps in the boarding used to seal it. She lost one of her slippers, staggering on with one bare foot scraping against the rough, dusty flooring. But when eventually she reached the window, the cracks in the boarding were too small for her to see much of what lay outside, nothing but the dismal light and a steady evening drizzle that had returned in place of the earlier sunshine. It fell from the sky like the tears that were falling inside her.

"Remember Hasan. Think of Hasan."

It was her mantra. His baby face was visible in her mind's eye, his baby chuckle ringing in her ears. Jamil no longer mattered to her; she would see him in hell for what he had done. But first she must escape.

Amongst the dust and debris around her feet she caught sight of something shiny. Squinting in the dim light she made out the jagged edge of a broken bottle glinting in contrast to the darkness around it. She shuffled towards it and shunted it over by the wall, then turning with her back against the brickwork, she slid herself slowly and painfully down to the floor to sit beside the bottle, to where she could reach it with her hands.

Grasping it tight in her fingers, she rubbed it against the rope around her wrists in slow, painstaking movements, pausing at intervals to rest when her hands, rubbed raw by the rope, became too sore and painful. Now and then she caught her flesh with the jagged edge and felt the sting of a cut and the stickiness of blood on her fingers. Tears rolled down her cheeks and fear constricted her chest. A rat scuttled across the floor in front of her. She stifled a shriek in her throat and for a moment she was back in the earthquake. The rats had been everywhere. Everywhere. And they frightened her. In panic she struggled to rise to her feet still clutching the bottle in her hand. Pushing her back against the wall and digging her feet against the ground she rose little by little.

By the time she had managed to sever the rope her world was in darkness apart from the silvery light from a full moon that streaked through the gaps in the boarding, as and when it emerged between the rainclouds. She tore the tape from her mouth with a cry as it ripped the skin of her lips. They stung and the wetness of blood on her hands brushed on her chin. But she did not care - at least now she was almost free, at least she had a chance. She crouched down to untie the rope around her feet. Expecting her collection and disposal to be within hours and while she was still weak from the drugs, Jamil had been careless in his binding so it took her only minutes to free herself completely. Now exhausted and frightened but watchful for the sound of approaching inhumanity, she needed time to recover before moving on. She looked for a place to rest in the deepening darkness.

******

Outside the door of Sofiya's room Sapphire stood listening trying to guage what was happening inside. The crashing and banging that had previously been in progress had now subsided as Sofiya considered her next move. She sat on the bed planning.

"I must get free. I must find Anastasiya."

She had promised their late mother to care for her younger sister and she had let them both down. It had been she, Sofiya, who had persuaded Anastasiya to come to England now; it had been she who had insisted they come now rather than wait until 2014 when entry would be unrestricted.

"It is too long to wait," she had told her sister. "How are we to live on the pittance we earn here for all that time? In England we can earn good money, have a good life. If we use Mama's savings to get to England we can get good jobs. Let us go now, before all the others. We can get the best work before them. We both have a little English. It is enough."

Anastasiya had been reluctant.

"But if we fail Mama's savings will be gone; these people charge a lot of money. If we are stopped at the border they will send us back and it will all have been for nothing. If we wait it will be easier to get in the country."

"No, Mama's savings will soon be gone anyway. We do not earn enough here to live without them. Let us go now."

At last Anastasiya had agreed. Now where was she? Sofiya had to find her. This was not the life she had envisaged for either of them, sex slaves for the benefit of these perverted people. What had happened to her with that pig of a man was bad enough but it must not happen to her younger sister. Somehow she must protect her, if she was not too late already. But how? First she must escape and then she would have to find her. These were her problems and right now she had no solutions.

The room around her was in chaos. The door was barricaded, the bedhead wedged resolutely under the door handle. She had refused a repeat of the other night when that animal of a man had come and seduced her.

"Sofiya, open the door."

"No. I will not do it. That man will not touch me again, I swear."

Sapphire's tone was dispassionate.

"Sofiya, it will happen. There is no escaping it. Next time he comes they will make you. You will soon get used to it. It's nothing, just sex, that's all. What's the big deal?"

"Not to me. It is wrong. You make me dirty. I want my sister. What have you done with her?"

"Look, I have food here – and drink. You need to keep yourself ok. I will ask Sadie about your sister. Now open the door."

"No."

Time was marching on and Sapphire had duties to perform. She was out of patience with this girl who was causing her so much trouble. She muttered an oath and left the landing to return downstairs to telephone Sadie.

"There's nothing I can do, Sadie. She's wedged something under the door handle so the door won't budge. She's a bloody nuisance. But it's unsettling for the other girls. They're asking what's going on. I'll have a full scale revolt on my hands at this rate."

"We're having the same problem here with the sister. I'm going to fetch your girl here and put them together for the time being. If they're both in the same room we only have to deal with one problem, not two. They'll have to eat and drink soon. When they do we'll deal with it. Thank God for rohipnol."

"When will you come?"

"As soon as Ebony's free to take over for me. Shouldn't be long. Her Client will be leaving shortly."

"Good. You;lll be here soon then."

"Yes. Soon."

Sofiya had returned to pondering her predicament. She needed to get out of this room somehow and without interference from this woman Sapphire, who had remonstrated with her, then tried to cajole her. It all amounted to the same. The woman was simply trying to break down her resistance. Sofiya had not eaten for twenty four hours and the only liquid that had passed her lips had been sips from the remnants of a bottle of water in the only bag of her possessions they had allowed her to keep. Sapphire had taken everything else, especially the passport that had cost such a lot of money and most of her clothes. But in her make-up bag she had a penknife, part of what she called her 'survival kit'. Right now that one piece of equipment might prove a life-saver. She was trying to form a plan when Sadie's voice at the door jolted her out of her thoughts.

"Sofiya, this is Sadie. Open this door right now. I am here to take you to your sister."

Sofiya considered. It could be a trap but she could not ignore a chance to find Ana. She pushed the bed away from the door and heard Sadie turn the key. The door opened to reveal the woman before her with a thunderous expression.

"Get your things and hurry. I've enough to do without the trouble you've caused me."

Gathering her few possessions together quickly and stuffing them into her shoulder bag, Sofiya complied.

"Right. Follow me – and no funny business if you want to see that sister of yours again, do you hear me?"

Sofiya nodded. She believed her. Ushered into Sadie's car, they sped through town until pulling up outside the strip club where Sadie based her business. A brash neon sign flashed on and off above the door. Indicating an alleyway that ran down the side of the building, Sadie barked her instructions.

"This way."

Sofiya walked ahead of her to a door towards the rear.

Unlocking the door, Sadie pushed Sofiya inside and standing at the bottom of a staircase ahead of them, she called to Ebony, who appeared from a door to the side of them with a tray.

"Ah, good. You got it then," and she took the tray holding two boxes of KFC and two bottles of water.

"Up you go," she told Sofiya.

At the top of two flights of stairs Sadie opened the door to a sparsely furnished attic room and pushed Sofiya inside.

Following behind her, she closed and locked the door. Anastasiya looked up fearfully from where she sat on one of the beds, then gasped in relief as she saw her Sofiya. The sisters ran to each other, babbling in their native tongue.

"Oh, Ana. You look terrible. What have they done to you?" Anastasiya's eyes were puffed from crying and black smudges of mascara stained her pasty skin. Her hair and clothes were dishevelled, crumpled and sweaty. She had refused to wash and change since arriving, refused to wear the clothes Sadie had given her, guessing the implication.

"Nothing",she said. "I would not let them, Sof. I would do nothing they told me. These are bad people. We must get away from them."

Sadie interrupted their reunion.

"Now, look here, you two. I don't think you understand your situation. You'd better get a few things straight. And don't pretend you don't understand me. Your English is good enough. From tomorrow you will toe the line and do as you're told. Because if you don't things will get very nasty for you. You don't seem to realise how well you'll be treated here. If you don't behave then you'll be sold off to the lower end of the market, some pimp or the other who'll lock you in a room and just send in one man after another. Separate rooms, that is. You wouldn't see each other. And the men - all the worst types. No-one would bother what they did to you. You're lucky you're here so better get on with it. Understand?"

She paused to allow the impact of her words to sink in. The two girls stood silent before her, offering no response. They had grasped the main of her rant.

"Now, I'm going to leave you to think things over tonight. See here; I've brought you food and drink. But I'll be back in the morning expecting some co-operation. It's up to you," and she left, slamming and locking the door behind her.

Anastasiya broke into tears and hugged her sister.

"What are we going to do?"

"Oh, Ana. I'm so sorry I brought you to this."

Journey into Darkness

"At least we are together, Sof. I have missed you so much," and the tears cascaded down her cheeks.

"We have to get out of here, Ana. I will not do what they want. That man - the foreign one we met when we arrived. He drugged and raped me and he tried to come back last night. I refused and locked myself in my room. I will not do it. Let's eat and drink while we think about it. I am so hungry and we need our strength to escape."

She gulped the water greedily in her thirst then bit into a piece of chicken as she looked around the room. There were two single beds against the wall on the one side, on one of which Ana had been sitting when they entered and in which she had clearly slept, if she had slept at all. Against the opposite wall was an old toilet and washbasin with a towel hung on the rail, a rusting old radiator and the carpet looked aged and threadbare in places. No personal items were to be seen at all. The room, it seemed, had been used to for the same purpose before, like a prison cell to hold the reluctant. She crossed to the dormer window and looked down on the view outside.

"Ana, look. See on the floor below. There's a fire escape. If we can get down to that ..."

Anastasiya joined her sister at the window.

"There's a drainpipe at the side – look. Do you think we could reach it?"

"What, to climb down, do you mean?"

Anastasiya nodded.

"Maybe, but we have to get out there first and this window is locked."

They were silent for a moment, consuming the remainder of the chicken. Sofiya prodded the frame of the window with her finger.

"This is made of wood, Ana, and the wood's soft like it's going rotten. I still have my penknife. Maybe we could dig out the lock?"

"We can try. And then what do we do?"

"Do you still have the address that man back home gave us?"

"Yes, in my purse – here," and Ana took out a paper folded

neatly in the side pocket of her wallet.

"And the money?"

"Yes. I keep it in my bra," and she drew from her bra a £20. note folded small. Do you have yours?"

"No. They found it and took it from me, but yours should be enough. The address is here in London, in N e w C r o s s," she read carefully. "We should be able to get to it."

They talked through a plan for the morning.

******

The clock on the cooker gave a faint click as the minutes flicked over to 19.05 and expecting Martin at any moment, Helen finished laying the table. The ringing of the doorbell came with perfect timing.

"Can I do anything to help?"

"You can open the wine if you like. There's white or rose in the 'fridge and red in the rack. Whatever's your preference."

"I'm a red man myself. I know Prosecco's the thing these days but I still prefer a red. Ok with you?"

"Yes, red's fine."

Martin checked the bottles in the rack while Helen checked the spaghetti.

"Ah, a Chilean. That will do nicely. I'm really sorry, Helen. I meant to bring some but to be honest I was running a bit late and forgot."

"Busy day?"

"You could say that! The Gunners were playing at home. It's always a bit lively when there's a home game."

"Drinking and celebrating, I suppose."

"Well, drunk anyway, either to celebrate or to drown their sorrows. Makes no difference either way. If I had a tenner for every time I've been told 'we was robbed' I'd be booking a holiday in the Bahamas. So all thought of wine flew out of my head, I'm afraid."

"Oh, it's no problem. Are you a fan?"

"What, of footie, do you mean?"

Helen nodded.

"God, no. I'm not really a sporting man. Like to watch the tennis when the grand slams are on but that's about the size of it."

"Well, no worries about the wine. I'm sure you and Jules will return the compliment some time. The opener's in the drawer there."

"Not sure about that one, Helen. I'm not sure where Jules and I are heading at the moment."

"Really? Oh, Martin, you surprise me. You've been together for so long. What's the problem?"

"I'm not sure. Maybe that's it. Just that we've been together for so long. School-hood sweethearts and all that. But I feel we're moving in different directions. Drifting apart. Jules seems preoccupied with her own life and friends - and my job, well, you know what it's like being a policeman. It can take over so much of your life."

"Do you feel you're being pushed into making a choice?"

"A bit. Do I address what I see as a problem or ignore it as just par for the course? That's the question. I don't know whether Jules is feeling the same. Or whether she has already made her decision and just wants out. I've broached the subject of children but she always ducks the issue. We used to talk about having a family one day, once our careers were established. But she avoids the subject these days."

"You mean, you want to start a family and she doesn't?

"Yes, I do. I don't know whether she's changed her mind about having children or whether she just doesn't want them with me."

"Well, it sounds to me like you've stopped talking to each other. So you need to have this conversation with Jules, then, don't you? That's the first move."

"How did you cope, Helen? When you and Steve were going through it?"

"Oh, well, that was different, wasn't it? Steve was seeing

someone else. He was besotted. There was little I could do to combat that. Our relationship was long-standing, like yours is with Jules. We'd become comfortable; familiar. It was a case of the grass being greener. The new relationship was exciting. It had to run its course one way or the other. And now, of course, she's pregnant so right or wrong the die is cast."

"That must be hard for you, Helen? Did you want children?"

"It is and I did. But he kept saying he wasn't ready. Same old story really."

Helen switched from a subject that was painful.

"Do you think there's anyone else involved where you and Jules are concerned?"

Martin was thoughtful.

"No. At least I don't think so. But then, as the saying goes, perhaps I'll be the last to know."

"Well, whatever's going on between you two, I hope you manage to sort it out and stay together. I've always thought you the ideal couple. What about the job? Any plans there? CID? Promotion."

"Not CID for me, I think. I like uniformed. I like just being the local bobby, part of the community. You get to know people and they you. It isn't all bad stuff. Does that sound unambitious of me? I wonder whether that's something Jules thinks of me."

"No, not at all. We don't all want to be the boss at the top of the tree. It's always seemed to me to be a bit of a lonely place. I'm like you; I like being involved at grass roots level. Helping everyday people in their everyday lives."

Helen placed a bowl of spaghetti bolognaise on the ready-laid table, slid a basket of garlic bread by its side and a dish of parmesan.

"Come on, supper's ready. Hungry?"

"Ravenous. It smells wonderful. But you always were a good cook."

"There's a crumble for pud. You always liked crumble as a kid, I remember."

"I still do. Couldn't be better."

They sat together in comfortable conversation, demolishing the supper and washing it down with the wine.

"So - tell me about this mum of yours, then."

"Her name's Katya. She and her husband are both Turkish."

"The abusive husband. Are you sure about that? You believe her?"

"Oh, yes. I've seen the damage. She denied it at first, said she was accident prone; the usual excuses. But eventually she admitted it to me on a visit. It's a familiar story, Martin. I've seen it before. So have you. Always excusing him; blaming herself; thinking that if she improved her behaviour things will go back to the days of wine and roses."

Martin nodded his understanding.

"Yeah, you're right. It's familiar. But why do you think something's happened to her?"

"Well, she didn't come to the clinic when I'd asked her so I decided to call round at the house. Casually, so to speak, in case the husband was at home. I knocked several times but there was no reply."

"Well, like I said before, maybe she was out shopping or something."

"Yeah, I realised that, Martin; that she could be out somewhere. Of course she could. But it was still niggling at me, so I looked through the letterbox. Hasan's pushchair was still in the hall with his outdoor suit on top."

"Hasan?"

"The baby. He's 5 months old. Katya's a very diligent mother. She would never take him out in weather like this unless it was really necessary and certainly not without his warm suit; even if she was in the car with her husband, which is unlikely. From what she's told me he never takes her anywhere. She's virtually a prisoner in that house."

"The husband. What does he do?"

"He's an immigration officer."

"Ever met him?"

73

"Only the once. He was very abrupt; dismissive. As though he disapproved of my presence."

"Of you or your job, do you think?"

"Oh, no, not of the job, I don't think. He's always insisted to Katya that she brings Hasan for his regular checks and immunisation. So it must be me."

"There's no sign of abuse where the baby's concerned then?" Helen shook her head emphatically.

"No, no. Hasan's thriving. I'm not at all worried in that respect."

Martin was thoughtful for a moment.

"Well, some of this could be down to cultural attitude, don't you think? His manner towards you – a woman in a position of authority? Not of the abuse. That's just criminality and nothing excuses that."

"Maybe, though he's been in this country for some time. He should be used to our culture by now. But I'm not bothered about his attitude towards me. I meet all sorts in my job, same as you do. You grow a thick skin when you're exposed to the public in the course of your work, don't you? It's Katya I'm concerned for. She started to tell me one day - where I come from- as though where she comes from it's ok for a man to beat his wife. But then she stopped, as if she was embarrassed to say it. Her injuries haven't been light, Martin. And they seem to be escalating, which as we both know is the usual pattern. At first it was bruising; on her arms as though she had been restrained roughly. Then a split lip or two. When she finally admitted to me that it was Jamil physically abusing her she was in pain from bruised ribs. Cultural or not, in this country we don't tolerate abuse of any kind, do we?"

Martin gave an ironic snort.

"Well, in theory. But in the light of recent events I'm not sure this country can claim any moral high ground in the treatment of women. Particularly young women. Or of young people of either sex, come to that. All these high profile celebrity sex abuse cases against minors. And the cover-ups. Then there have been all the revelations about the Catholic Church over decades."

"Mmmm. More cover-ups there."

"And that's only the stuff we know about. Then there's all this sex slavery business. Who knows how much more goes on behind closed doors. Some of the things I've seen, Helen! I tell you, there are days when I hardly recognise the society I thought I lived in. Fact is, Helen, we have to take responsibility for our own society before we criticise others. Get over this obsession with power and celebrity that means anyone in a position of influence can get away with blue murder."

"Oh, yes. I agree there. It's sad the way people idolise celebrity, or so called celebrity. I don't know who half of them are, people who seem to have done nothing to earn the label. But I see it all the time with young mums who have to dress their baby in designer clothing, all the latest trends. Like they're dressing a doll. And they're usually mums who can't really afford it anyway. Nearly every week some celebrity or other brings out a new perfume or a new range of designer clothing based on what they dress Mixie Trixie in, or whatever they've called the latest edition to their family. It's hard work sometimes trying to get over the message that the important thing is basic care, never mind the frills."

"Oh, don't get me started on the celebrity thing. I've had this conversation with Jules when she wants the latest designer handbag that I can't afford on a policeman's pay. What is it with women and handbags?"

Helen grinned.

"Mars and Venus heh?" she thought.

"Well, I don't know what the answer is," she went on. "Only that we need to try even harder to protect the vulnerable. Social workers and the care industry all do their best but with constant cuts and targets to achieve, it's an uphill struggle. It's no wonder some slip through the net."

Martin grinned.

"You'd hold your own well on a soap box, Hel."

Helen laughed.

"You too. We sound like our parents, don't we? Do you remember the conversations at our family get togethers? Putting the world to rights?"

"Oh, God, yes. I do. And we used to take the mickey out of them. Oh, dear. Must be an age thing. The final proof that we're getting older."

"Oh, don't. Don't. I'm suddenly feeling ancient."

They groaned and laughed together.

"But getting back to your young mum, you know as well as I do that unless she's prepared to make a complaint against him we're unable to do anything. I *will* check with the hospitals, though. Just to put your mind at rest on that score. What's her full name?"

"Hussein. Katya Hussein."

"And her husband is Jamil Hussein."

"Yes."

"I'll run a check on him, too. See if he's got any form."

"Thanks, Martin. And I'll keep an eye out for her. I'll call at the house again on Monday. And if she's ok, if it's just me being paranoid – I'll let you know."

"Great. Well, I'd better be off. Thanks for the supper, Helen. Good as ever. And it's been great to talk. We really should do this more often. Busy lives are no excuse."

"That would be lovely, Martin. See you soon."

******

Jamil was exhausted. Hasan had been fretful and settling him to sleep had been difficult. Producing a dirty nappy that had set his father a challenge, Hasan at last was settled in his cot and close to sleeping. Scrubbing his hands once the nappy was suitably disposed of, Jamil wafted an air freshener around the room in irritation.

"Women's work," he grumbled. "This is for women to do, not me."

"Have to get used to it," his companion taunted. "At least

when he is at home."

Jamil answered the ring of the doorbell before slumping onto the sofa with a take-away just arrived at the door. His tiredness was exacerbated by anxiety in the absence of a call from Ross. Surely the man had taken Katya by now so why had he not rung as promised? He tried Ross's number without success; just a message telling him that the mobile was currently unavailable. His companion reassured him.

There's probably a simple explanation. Try again in the morning. Be patient and don't panic. The morning will bring its own solutions. Things always look better in the morning."

All the same, he was edgy in his impatience and it irked him that the man had not kept his word, causing anxiety in his neglect. What if he had not kept his word with Katya? What if he had failed to do the job? Tomorrow, he decided, he must know for sure.

Chapter Seven

Sunday, 14th September – am

Jamil had tossed and turned all night. It was still strange without Katya's presence and his annoyance with Ross had niggled at him, so despite his tiredness, sleep had not come easily. When at last it did come, it was punctuated by his spectres from the past and questions from the present. By the time he was woken by Hasan, he could not know that events already unfolding were rapidly spiralling beyond control. He tried Ross's number once more and receiving the same message that the mobile was not available, he decided that a visit to the warehouse to check the job was done was essential. First he would take Hasan to Mina and then go on from there.

******

Light was already breaking by the time that Sofiya was able to loosen the lock on the window. Time was short. She and Ana had taken it in turns to dig out the wood around it, their hands and fingers aching and sore from the effort but determination carrying them on. In between their turn, each had washed at the basin in the room and changed into clean clothing from the little they had been allowed to keep, doing their best with appearances now suffering from lack of attention and facilities. "I feel such a mess, Sof. I've done my best but I need a shower and my hair really, really needs washing. People will look at us like we're tramps or something. And when we get to New Cross, what will they think of us?"
"Don't worry. They will expect us to look untidy from the journey. They will have seen it before. At least we're cleaner now we've washed a little. It was lucky someone left a piece of soap in the basin. Otherwise we would have had nothing."
"Who do you think that was? The last person they kept shut up in this room like a prisoner?"

"I'd rather not think about it, Ana. It's all too much."

Stuffing essentials into their shoulder bags and the pockets of their jeans and jackets, toothpaste and brushes, underwear, whatever they could carry, their money and the contact address, with the window opened, they were ready to go. The sight of the task ahead of them made them gulp.

"Ana, we will have to be very careful. Are you sure you can reach across to that pipe from here? Your legs are not as long as mine."

"I will do it, Sof. I have to. I will do it."

"Let me go first, then. You can watch me to see how I do it." Sofiya climbed onto the window ledge, her arms hooked around the frame to steady her body. Her shoulder bag swung behind her threatening to destabilise her and she balanced on the ledge to unhook it from her shoulder and drop it to the ground. She tried again, stretching her right arm and leg towards the pipe. In the dampness of the morning, the pipe was slippery and it took her several attempts to successfully wrap the calf of her leg around it. With a deep breath and a word of prayer and breathing hard, she swung herself across and wrapped herself around the pipe, arms clinging tight and her thighs clenched around it. Moving steadily down the pipe until level with the fire escape, she swung across to stand on the top platform. Covering her fear, she looked up at Ana with a smile.

"Ok, Ana. Do you think you can do it?"

"I have to. I will."

"You're very brave, Ana. Come on, I will do my best to help you. Throw your bag to the ground first."

The bag hit the ground with a soft thud and they paused, anxious that the noise had been heard by a light sleeper but there was no other sound, no hint of anyone disturbing. The quiet calm of sleeping remained around them.

"Come on, then. Come."

Sofiya watched, heart in her mouth, as her sister followed her example with surprising ease, adrenalin firing her into action. They stood on the platform of the fire escape and hugged in relief.

"Come on. We must hurry."

Shoes in hand, they padded softly to the ground.

Once in the street, the two girls rushed hand in hand away from the club with no idea where they were heading. A faint mist tinged the still, quiet air with dampness and there were few people about, just a few stragglers from the night's revelry and a lonely road-sweeper doing his rounds. At the corner with the next side street they paused.

"Which way?"

"It doesn't matter, Ana. Just run; as long as we get around a corner out of sight," and Sofiya pulled her sister down the side street. They repeated the tactic several times until they were sure there was some distance between them and the place of their imprisonment, then paused again to consider the best way to go.

"Look, Ana. Down there. There's a sign. Let's go and see what it says."

They peered up at the large green sign to see if New Cross was listed as a destination but it was not there.

"Sofiya, look . That sign. That must mean station. Why not go there and then we can find out how to get to New Cross?"

"Yes, good idea. Let's go," and still hand in hand they made their way towards Euston.

The station concourse was not yet crowded in the early morning hour. The town had not yet woken. A loudspeaker boomed a barely audible announcement that they struggled to understand. The girls brushed the dampness from their shoulders and tidied the now bedraggled hair, glancing around them for a clue as to the direction they must take.

"We will have to ask. See over there at that window. It says 'Information'."

Ana interrupted her sister's enthusiasm to rush on.

"Sof, can we sit down for a minute? I'm so tired. And I'm cold. I can smell coffee. If we had a hot cup of coffee I think I would feel better."

"Alright. But we mustn't stay too long. The sooner we get to New Cross the better. Look, you sit there on that seat and look after our bags. Give me the money. I'll go and get coffee."

As they sipped their coffee, the girls became aware of two youths hovering close by, one who looked English, the other foreign, maybe Asian or of Arabic extraction. The English one nudged his colleague forward.

"Go on. They don't look English. You might have the lingo."
Catching their eye, the youth came closer, smiling and speaking to them in a friendly manner.

"Hi, girls. You look lost. Is there something I can do to help you?"

"We're fine," Sofiya told him abruptly. "Thank you but we not need your help."

"Are you sure? Look, I don't want to alarm you. I just thought …. "

"Please go away. Leave us alone," insisted Sofiya sharply.
Ana pressed close to her sister.

"Heh, look, girls, I'm only trying to help you, yeah? My friend, he's local. He knows everything around here. If you're lost he's …. "

"We not lost. Leave us alone."

Across at the information window, someone was watching. He reached for a telephone close by and buzzed security.

"Morning, Tom. Look, there's a couple of young girls down on the platform here. Look like they've been up all night. Lost maybe. They're being hassled by two of those guys you wanted us to keep an eye on. Thought I'd better let you know."

"Ok, Reg. Thanks for letting me know. I'll send a couple of our lads over straight away."

Officers from the Transport Police approached. The young man edged away from the girls and quietly melted into the background behind a group of Japanese tourists now assembling on the platform with their guide. His colleague made off rapidly in a different direction.

"Morning, girls," one of the policemen addressed them. "Everything alright?"

Sofiya nodded without a word, not wishing to hold their attention but the officers were not to be denied.

"Where are you two off to then?"

"We need go to New Cross."

"New Cross? That's a strange destination. Not tourists then? You work there?"

Sofiya shook her head.

"We visit friends," she answered with reluctance.

The two officers exchanged glances.

"Ok, well maybe we can help you there, Miss … ah?"

"Sofiya," she said, again reluctantly, wondering how she could bring to an end this unwanted conversation.

"Sofiya, that's a pretty name. And who's this with you?"

"Sister. Ana."

"Ana. So another pretty name. And where are you and your sister from then, Sofiya?"

Sofiya looked at the officer with a blank expression.

"Your home? What country are you from?"

"Romania."

"Romanian, huh. Ok. Do you have a passport on you, Sofiya? An ID card perhaps?"

Sofiya gave a sigh.

"At 'otel," she replied after a moment. Ana remained silent beside her.

"And which hotel would that be then? Since you're not tourists."

Sofiya stumbled for words.

"I not remember the name," and turning to Ana she spoke in Romanian, asking her, "Quick, Ana. Quick. Think of a hotel name."

"'Ilton," whispered Ana, the only London hotel she knew of., remembered from a magazine back home. Sofiya turned back to face the officers.

"'Ilton," she replied. "'Ilton 'Otel."

The officers exchanged glances and then turned sideways to the girls and discussed between them.

"From the Hilton to New Cross, heh. Well, either they've had a damned good night on the tiles or they're lying and I know what I think. What about you?" said one.

His colleague nodded and replied.

"Yeah, something not right here. I think we should look into this a bit closer," and he turned to Sofiya.

"We'd like you and your sister to come with us please. Bring your bags along. We'll see what we can do to help you."

The girls looked alarmed. The policemen's manner seemed kind enough but even so; they were worried.

"Why?" Sofiya protested with alarm. "We just need go to New Cross. Our friends waiting. We not need help – really not. We just have coffee while we wait train."

"Yes, all in good time, miss. I understand that. But first you come with us. There's no need to worry. We're policemen. You'll be quite safe," and he produced his ID to put her mind at ease.

With no other option apparent but with continuing reluctance, the girls collected their bags together and accompanied the officers across the concourse.

******

The sight of the empty room and the open window sent Sadie into a spin.

"Fucking hell," she breathed. "If they get picked up we could all be in trouble."

She examined the lock from the window now abandoned on the floor.

"How the fuck....?"

She pondered whether she should ring Jamil to warn him. He would be furious and a part of her was just a little reluctant to incur his wrath. She closed and locked the door behind her and rushed down the stairs, calling Ebony as she went. In her office on the ground floor, she sat back in her chair behind the desk and lit a cigarette.

"This fucking old building. Rotting. Rotting all over the place. But how did they do that to the window?"

At the knock on the door, she barked an order to enter. Her demeanour put Ebony on guard.

"The girls, they've gone."

Ebony gasped.

"But how? The door was locked."

"The window. They climbed out of the window. They must have had a knife or something to dig out the lock. Did you check their bags when they arrived?"

"Yes. Really I did. I saw nothing."

"Well, they're gone. You say nothing to anyone, do you understand?"

Ebony nodded, the colour draining from her face. Sadie was angry. She was not pleasant when she was angry and the anger could be directed at her.

"When? How long have they been gone?"

"I have no idea."

Sadie looked at her watch.

"8.30 now. I think it gets light about half past six so I suppose they wouldn't have gone much before that. But they could be anywhere by now."

She drew hard on her cigarette, thinking desperately of any course of action she could take for damage limitation but no solution came. She had their passports and the money the girl Sofiya had had with her. So where could they go? They were illegal so the police were an unlikely destination. Nowhere other than to be picked up on the streets by a pimp.

"Well, so be it," she thought. "They'll soon discover how

pointless that's been."

"Go and get on with what you were doing.," she told Ebony.
"And mind you keep your mouth shut."

Once on her own, Sadie considered once more the question of
whether she should ring Jamil. On balance she decided his
anger now would be better than his anger later should the
police arrive on their doorstep, unlikely though that may be.
She rang his mobile, but was relieved when her call was
ignored.

"I'll try again later. It's his own fault if he doesn't answer his
fucking 'phone."

Raised from her sleep tousled and heavy-eyed, Ebony left the
office stunned at the news but admiring of the girls's courage.
She wished she had found the courage herself. A runaway at
15, escaping an abusive drink-addicted mother, she had been
easy prey. No-one had taken the trouble to report her missing.
In a traumatised and vulnerable state, her self-esteem non-
existent, it had taken little time and effort on the part of the
unscrupulous to pick her up on the street. She had believed the
promises of help and a rosy future, barely noticed the transition
from waitress to stripping, from stripping to prostitution. Her
skin was dark and smooth, her hair glossy with the crinkled
curl of her race. She had eyes as dark as night that glowed
from the whites around them, a slim body and long slender legs
like an athlete. With little effort and the smallest of investment
on clothes and cosmetic polishing, she'd been turned into an
exotic fantasy figure that wetted the lustful male appetite.
Ebony was the obvious name to complete the transformation.

Now two years on, she was one of Sadie's busiest girls. If she
had ever thought of going home, she had dismissed the thought
as quickly as it had come. She couldn't go home. There was
no-one at home who gave a damn. Not her mother. Her
mother wouldn't care if she were alive or dead, if she was still
alive herself, that was. Maybe her mother was dead by now,
her brain and body imploded in a drink-induced frenzy. Ebony

knew she had a safety and security of sorts with Sadie. Sadie kept her clients clean, no bad stuff, no violence. She had bouncers on the door ready and ever-willing to dispense punishment to anyone over-stepping the mark. There were one or two that could be a bit rough and over demanding who had been given a warning but mostly they were just sad inadequates unable to satisfy their needs at home. But she also had a label now. She was a prostitute, a whore; and her label held her trapped outside the life she had once dreamed of.

She had been a talented student at school before her home situation had traumatised her into academic impotence. Her teachers had envisaged a future place at art school, an artistic career that would offer her exciting options. But she had given up believing, bombarded by her mother's constant derision, so that was all gone now. And there would be no loving husband, no children, for what decent man would want for his wife what she had become? So she performed each day the role that life had allotted her, emotionless, de-sensitized to the sordid monotony of the abuse of her body, uncaring of her tomorrow for what promise of hope did tomorrow offer her? Good for these girls that they had found such courage.

"Go, girls," she whispered. "Go. Run as fast as you can. And please God keep you safe."

Chapter Eight

Sunday, 14th September – pm

In the warehouse Katya was searching for an exit route. She had slept fitfully through the night, darkness preventing any other course of action but fear had woken her often and she felt jaded from sleep deprivation, from the effects of the drugs and the lack of food and water. Her whole body felt weak. She had found the holdall left by Jamil and opened it to see what was inside. The sight of all the money confirmed what she had already come to believe; that he was paying someone to get rid of her.

"Such a coward, Jamil," she ranted. "Not man enough to do it yourself, only to slap and hit but not to do the whole thing, not to see my face in front of you as you do it. No, not that."
The holdall was evidence so she knew she must take it with her to the police, her first course of action once free. She puffed in disgust, her initial shock gone now, her survival instinct firmly in control. She had survived worse than this in the past, she told herself.; this would not defeat her. Rising to her feet she looked around her.

At the far end of the room was a staircase to an upper floor of rooms, what she supposed had been offices when the warehouse had been in use. There was light there that suggested an opening, maybe a door or a window. Taking the holdall with her she climbed the stairs looking for a window that was not boarded and found one, but it was locked. Below it was the sloping roof of a single-storey extension that looked like some sort of outhouse. Looking around for a tool to prise open the window or a stone to break the glass, she was surprised by the sound of the door downstairs being opened. She caught her breath with a gasp. Grabbing the holdall, she hid behind the door, peering through the slit between the hinged door and the architrave. Light from outside silhouetted a figure in the downstairs doorway but the identity of the visitor was not clear until they walked forward. Then she recognised the gait, she knew the figure. It was Jamil. Her breathing constricted by fear, she watched as he crossed to where he had left her. She remembered the pieces of rope she had cut from her wrists and taken from her ankles. They were left on the floor with the tape from her mouth but a little apart from where she had lain. She prayed that he would not notice them amongst the other debris. She held her breath for what seemed like an eternity, struggling not to make a sound in her anxiety.

Downstairs Jamil crossed to the place where he had placed his unconscious wife. With Hasan left with Mina, he had been impatient to check that all had gone to plan. The warehouse seemed silent and empty with nothing to arouse suspicion, no movement other than leaves blown in by the breeze from the now open door scuttling across the floor.

"Gone," he murmured with satisfaction. "She is gone. And the holdall. It must be done," and confident of a successful conclusion, he turned and returned to his car, closing the doors with a clang that echoed across the empty space and padlocking the outer door behind him.

"There, I told you," said his companion. "I told you everything would be alright."

"Yes, you were right," he replied. "You were right. You're always right."

From her hiding place upstairs, Katya watched him leave. She breathed a sigh of relief. Her heart was pounding and she felt weaker than ever from the sudden fear of discovery. Calming herself, she concentrated once more on her plan, convinced now that she must act quickly just in case he or someone else returned.

"Think on, Jamil," she muttered. "I am coming to get you. I am coming."

A few moments on, sure that the sound of Jamil's car had

disappeared into the distance, she searched once more for a way of breaking open the window. Scrabbling amongst the debris littered across the floor, she found a sharp piece of concrete.

"This will do it, surely."

At the window she paused once more, listening, anxious that she was right and Jamil had really gone, worried that the noise might attract someone else of danger.

"You have to do it anyway. You must take the risk. You must. Do it. Go on. Do it."

She tapped the window twice with the concrete, too lightly to make an impact but enough for the concrete to crumple in her hand. She muttered her frustration and searched around her again. This time she found a jagged half brick. Taking a deep breath and turning her head sideways to avoid any splinters, she gave the glass a hefty clout. The centre of the pane shattered outwards leaving sharp shards of glass dangerously wedged around the sides of the frame. A welcome rush of air brushed her face, not cold, just a welcome newness that signalled another milestone towards freedom. It took her some time to carefully dislodge each shard of glass to leave the opening clear. She threw the holdall out onto the roof below and pulling herself up onto the bottom of the frame, sat astride it steadying herself ready to jump.

The roof below was wet from the overnight drizzle and the holdall had slid down to the guttering where it lodged and stuck. She breathed in the welcome air, felt the dampness of the morning on her dry, chafed lips. With both legs hanging over the outer wall, she lowered herself ready to move. With a quick word of prayer, she tried to slide herself slowly down to the roof below but once she let go of the window frame, she dropped like a stone, unable to control the speed of her fall. Her legs buckled under her as she hit the wet tiling and with a cry of pain as her ankle crunched, she bounced off the roof to the ground below, hitting her head on the guttering as she went. Losing consciousness, she lay motionless on the damp ground.

The stage was set for Jake and Ollie to make their entrance, for the whole circus of recovery to be set in motion before an unconscious Katya was transported to St Thomas' and WPC Holly installed by her side. And DCI Shakespeare and DS Gray were on the case.

******

The debris on the M25 from the previous day's accident had been cleared and investigations set in motion to notify the relatives of the deceased, thankfully in the carnage only Ross. Police officers calling at the print works in Romford were unable to get a reply to their knock on the door. From the vehicle's registration, they had done their homework, checked out the expected family of the deceased and being a Sunday morning had thought to find someone at home. In the absence of a response they tried the newsagent next door.

"We're trying to contact the family of Mr McKinnon," one of the officers explained. "Any idea when we might find someone at home?"

The newsagent shook his head.

"Lives there on his own, mate. Don't think 'e 'as any family."

"What about his son? Does he live here or is there another address for him?"

"Oh, it's the old man you're after! 'aven't seen the old man for years. They both lived 'ere at one time. We used to 'ear it all. Shouting. Banging about. Think the old man used to knock the son about a bit. But that stopped years ago. We thought the old man must've moved out. It's just the son on his own now."

"No-one else then? I gather the old man was a widower but – no woman on the scene?"

"With the son, you mean?"

The officer nodded.

"No, mate. No. Can't imagine any woman wantin' 'im",and the newsagent chuckled. "Not a very nice chap. Uncouth. Bit of a weirdo. Everyone round 'ere keeps their distance."

"So who could this woman be, then, do you think? Do you

recognise her at all? Ever seen her here?" the officer asked, producing a copy of the 'photo of Katya found crumpled and tossed about in Ross's car. The newsagent studied it carefully. "No, mate; no. Sorry, can't 'elp ya. Like I said, can't imagine any woman wantin' him. 'Specially a looker like 'er."

The officers agreed. Their only course of action was to force an entry. What they found inside was to trigger deeper investigation.

"Look at all this stuff. Hardcore porn. Looks like it's come from abroad. This is out of our remit, mate. I'll ring in for back-up."
Down in the cellar were more revelations.
"There's a laptop here. Perhaps we should take that back with us. And some samples of this disgusting stuff. This is much more than 'top shelf at the newsagents' stuff."
"No doubt about it. They'll get the techie boys on that. Who knows what they'll find judging by this lot. From what the neighbour said about him and what we've found here, this guy could be into anything. CID need to be taking a look at this one."

******

Katya's clothes were strewn across the bed where Jamil had thrown them from the wardrobe, the shoes on the floor beside it. He emptied the drawers she used in the chest and the bedside cabinet. Jerking open the black plastic bags torn from a roll in the kitchen, he bundled everything into them, muttering as he went.
"So many belongings, woman. Spending all my money."
He found the Pippa doll wrapped carefully in tissue paper and it unnerved him for a moment. A broken doll that seemed to stare at him accusingly.
"Where is my mistress? Have you broken her too?"
He dismissed his thoughts as fanciful, ridiculous, and threw the doll into the bag with disdain.

91

Next he moved to the dressing table where she kept her make-up and jewellery. Her engagement ring was in the box where she kept it and he recalled with horror that he had forgotten to remove the wedding ring from her finger.

"No matter. It is gone. She is gone. No-one will know."

Checking he had been thorough, he looked around the room. On the bedside table was a photograph, of himself and Katya on their wedding day. She was radiant, smiling - and those eyes. Again those beautiful, trusting eyes, the blonde hair, the fair colouring inherited from her English mother and so different from the girls in his village and the girls of his culture he had met here in London; so different, too, from Meryam. Somehow Katya had just been different to any other girl he had known. To Meryam, as different in looks as in temperament. Perhaps that was what had attracted him, Katya being bubbly but demure in her lovemaking, a coyness that in the beginning had prompted tenderness from him, until it had become a tedium. Meryam had been sassy, feisty, vibrant and exciting but dangerous. Her dark eyes would flash with passion, her long, glossy, chestnut tresses flounce with each toss of the head and sway of her curvaceous body and she would take the initiative without a blush. The lady and the harlot. From the photograph Katya's eyes held his own locked in their stare but he wrenched himself away. His stomach lurched. She had been his wife, the mother of his child and he had liked her once. Or maybe even loved her; he was not sure for what indeed was love between a man and a woman anyway. Sex he understood, the physical; but the emotional was something of a confusion. Love was bad for you. Love meant surrender, giving control of your life to someone else, a romantic image from the pages of a woman's novel. He had thought he loved Meryam but he had been wrong. Meryam had betrayed him, taken what he had to give and tossed it aside like an old shoe that had served its purpose. So what of Katya? It surely was not this thing people called love. But he was not finding it as easy to erase Katya from his life and his consciousness as he had expected. His companion came to his rescue. His companion reminded him.

"A woman. She was a woman, not to be trusted," it whispered. "You had to do it before she betrayed you. Women always betray you in the end. She gave you the son you wanted and now she's gone. You are free of her."

Snatching the photograph from the bedside table he thrust it into one of the black plastic bags.

He drove to the lock-up and dumped the bags in a corner at the back, out of the way until he could dispose of them later and closed and locked the door with a clang. Returning to the flat in the Docklands, he found Mina playing with Hasan in the lounge. The light was dying now, casting shadows eerily around the apartment. The scene invoked in him a mood of melancholy. He snapped on the lights to dismiss the gloom and trying to snap out of his malaise, he forced a smile and turned to his son. Hasan seemed at ease with Mina but as soon as he saw Jamil he became animated, gurgling and holding out his arms. Jamil picked him up with relief, hugging his boy to his chest.

"Baba has missed you," he told him, then turning to Mina, "he needs his tea. His jar of food needs warming. Do that and I will feed him?"

Mina disappeared at once into the kitchen. Jamil was pleased at her compliance, no word of dissent and a lack of irritating chit chat. She seemed content with her role.

Jamil fed his son, showing Mina their usual routine and together they made up a bottle of formula so she knew how much to give him and how Jamil liked it done. She changed Hasan's nappy and once ready, the boy was settled back into his car seat for the journey home.

"I will bring him again in the morning. Early. In the week when I am working he must stay with you at night but I will come every day to see him," Jamil told Mina as he left her alone for the evening. Pleased at the news, it was only after

Jamil had left that she remembered the key.
"Oh, no," she gasped. "Still no key," and she uttered a
curse in her native tongue.

At home, Jamil bathed Hasan and tried to settle him in his cot
but again the boy was fretful.
"Maybe you are missing your *Anne*, but that will soon go. It's
just you and *Baba* now."
"He will get over it," he assured himself. He will forget his
mother, it won't take long. And soon Hasan slept, tired by his
own fretfulness . Jamil made himself an omelette, then spent
the evening watching tv but he remained restless, the
unburdening he had expected to feel, free from Katya's
presence, eluding him. It was not as he had imagined it would
be. He still felt disorientated, strange in his own home. On his
'phone a missed call from Sadie commanded his attention but
in his disgruntled state of mind, he ignored it.
"Not now. I can't deal with that woman right now. Maybe in
the morning."

The house was becoming untidy, little things that he found
irritating, smudges of toothpaste on the bathroom basin, specks
on the mirror that he had meant to clean away but forgotten,
mail he had opened left scattered in odd places and Hasan's
laundry overflowing in the linen bin in his room. His crumpled
bed linen smelled stale from the sweat that drenched his
sleepless body and at 2 in the morning he stripped the bedding
replacing it with cool, clean covers, then showered and slipped
between the fresh smelling sheets. Once again he slept only
fitfully, half listening for cries through the baby alarm, but to
his relief, none came. Even so, the night was no improvement
on the one before, tossing and turning, a nauseous feeling
churning in his stomach each time he found himself facing
Katya's side of the bed.

He wondered how Ross had disposed of her. He had not asked
how it would be done. Had she regained consciousness and

known what was happening to her so that she knew he had
betrayed her? Was her end painful; was it quick? Try as he
might, he could not block the questions rising in his mind. Her
spectre now invaded his dreams like those of his mother and
his aunt, like the dark, taunting spirit of Meryam, a growing
company of detractors. His companion chided him.

"You should have done it yourself. Like Meryam. Then you
would have known, you wouldn't be tormenting yourself."

"No. I couldn't; not her."

"Why? Why not?"

Jamil could not answer.

"I don't know."

"Then stop tormenting yourself," his companion taunted.
"What good is this? You did what you had to do. She was
unhappy with you but now her pain is over. She is at peace.
Forget it."

It was well into the morning hours before he slept, only to be
woken at 6 am by Hasan's cries. He determined that he would
sell this house, leave behind its memories and make a new
start, perhaps in a smart new apartment. On his trips to the
Docklands he had been impressed by some of the buildings and
had a fancy for a penthouse overlooking the river. But in the
meantime, he needed a cleaner to take over the chores that
Katya's absence now left undone. He must move on.

Chapter Nine

Monday, 15th September

Jamil took Hasan to Mina early. He gave her a key and the pushchair, instructing her only to be out for about one hour as the weather had turned inclement, a sharp little wind now whipping around the corners in the drier air. He had considered long and hard whether he should let her outside of the apartment but had decided it was more risky not to than it was to do.

"You wrap him up well," he cautioned her. "It is cold outside."

"Not worry," she assured him. "I look after good."

The office was deserted when he arrived, deliberately early by design. No-one manned the main desk in reception as he entered, the security officer doing his rounds. The sound of movement and the opening and closing of doors told him the man was on the first floor. Taking care not to attract his attention, Jamil slipped quietly along the corridor to the central office. Wearing latex gloves he took the envelope with the £1000. from his jacket pocket and hid it under some papers in the bottom drawer of Jacob's desk. Satisfied it would be found on inspection, he went to his desk to retrieve the manifest, then paused. It was too risky. With the security guard patrolling, the noise of the shredder would be a give away and again he didn't have his briefcase. Impatient with his oversight, he left the same way he had come.

Across the road in the coffee bar, he watched as one by one the staff arrived, not least of all Len, then made a conspicuous entrance himself, seating himself flamboyantly at his desk. He had barely had time to be seated when Len called him for a progress report on the manifest from the ferry. Jamil gave him the information collected so far.

"I'm just finalising the last few enquiries, sir."

"Well, let me have a copy as quickly as possible. We need to start checking out some of these vehicles."

"Yes, sir. Right away."

Turning to leave Len's office, he paused in his step.

"What's the situation with Jacob?" he ventured.

"Nothing to report over the weekend. It seems he spent most of his time at his flat. But now that he's back at work things may develop. We must wait and see."

Jamil left Len's office with a smile on his lips. Things were developing nicely. He made for his desk, his mind focused on the task ahead.

"You look happy, Jamil. You been brown-nosing again?"

It was one of his colleagues, most of whom regarded Jamil with at the least reserve, at best contempt. Excluded these days from the after-work pints in the pub and the male chit chat, he was a routine target of their mistrust.

"He's such a creep," was the general consensus of opinion.

"You need to watch your back where Jamil's concerned."

"Yeah, drop his own grandmother in it to make himself look good."

Jamil faced the colleague, ignoring the invective. He leaned across and whispered into the man's ear.

"Perhaps you should be looking to your own business. If I were in your shoes," and he paused for maximum affect.

"Meaning?"

"Well, maybe you should be asking Jacob why he visits your wife while you're working."

The silence was rife with intrigue, the staff close by curious as to the content of Jamil's remark which, by the look on Steve's face, had been shattering. They had warned Steve before.

"You shouldn't goad him, Steve. He has the boss's ear; he can make life difficult for you."

Steve would not concede.

"He's a deceitful sycophant; makes me sick. I can't believe Len can't see through him. Well, I'm not going to cow tow to the likes of him."

"But he's the boss's deputy. He outranks you."

It made no difference. Steve Goss remained rebellious where Jamil was concerned but right now, he was pale and silent. He shot a glance across at Jacob, oblivious at his desk in the far corner, absorbed in a telephone conversation and unaware of the drama about to engulf him.

With a smirk of satisfaction, Jamil continued to his desk, his mind focused on the his own agenda – not least of all the need to destroy the original document still secreted in his desk. Despite the impression he gave to the contrary, frustration simmered beneath the surface in his anxiety to get the job done but with the office once more buzzing with his colleagues it would be far too risky to attempt right now. There were the likes of Steve Goss who he knew watched his every move, who would take delight in exposing anything questionable about him to Len.

"Why didn't you do it this morning? When the office was empty," his companion challenged.

He justified to himself that he had been focused on the more important task of Jacob. Perhaps it had been a mistake but it was too late now.

"I will do it. I will do it," he argued to himself. "When the coast is clear."

He resigned himself to waiting until after hours, concentrating on the task in hand for Len, but once again his motivation was hijacked. Len interrupted him in his task and called him into his office.

"You need to go to Camden station. Two girls were picked up at Euston last night that are thought to be illegal. No passports or ID. No real explanation why they're here. They've been held overnight at Camden to be interviewed this morning. Leave what you're doing right now and get over there."

Jamil left the office and hailed a cab.

******

The house again appeared silent and deserted as Helen stood at the entrance to the short paved forecourt. A small and brick-built semi with hedges at either side boundary, it was sheltered from the neighbours adding to the sense of isolation that Katya must feel. She was grateful that Jamil's car was absent, hoping Katya might be at home alone but again there was no response to her knock. She dipped into her pocket for her mobile to ring her cousin.

"Morning, Martin. It's me. I just wondered if you'd had chance to check up on Katya Hussein yet?"

"Hi, Helen. Yes. I checked the hospitals first thing yesterday morning, when I came on duty. Did it first thing before I got involved in anything else. Nothing to report, I'm afraid. Any luck with you?"

"No. I'm at the house now. I thought I'd come early so that if she was here I'd catch her before she went out anywhere, But there's no sign of anyone again. Not a sound. Did you check her husband?"

"Yes but again nothing. Clean as a whistle. Sorry, Helen, but I've not been much help, have I?"

"Oh, well, thanks for trying. We'll keep in touch, yeah?"

"Sure. I'll let you know if I hear anything."

"Love to Jules. Did she enjoy her hen do?"

Martin laughed.

"I think so. She hasn't really said much about it yet; still a bit hung over, I think. To be honest I think I'd rather not know the details."

******

Sofiya was sitting patiently in the interview room at the police station where she and her sister had been brought the previous evening. In a separate cell to her sister, exhaustion and the ataraxic effect of an unusually full stomach had taken over. They were safe, at least for the time being. She had slept

firmly until roused by a WPC who brought her toast and coffee.
"Where my sister?"
Anastasiya, she was told, had been taken to another room so
once more she and Ana were apart.
"We need to speak to each of you," the policeman told
her. But not together."
She tried to protest but soon realised that it was pointless. They
were illegal. They would be questioned and the stories each of
them gave subjected to scrutiny. And Ana had made it clear
that she wanted to return home.
"I am going to tell them everything, Sof. These bad people
need to be put in prison. I don't care if they send us home just
as long as we're together. I don't want to stay in this awful
country."
Sofiya had had no reply. She knew Ana was right to tell all
they knew and then no doubt they would be deported. But she
knew too that once home they would have nothing and life
would be hard. Now in the interview room she asked the
question again.
"Where my sister?"
Beside her, an interpreter did her best to reassure her but her
mood was sombre.
"Why are we waiting?" she asked in Romanian.
The interpreter replied.
"Someone is coming from the Border office. We have to wait
for them to sit in on the interview. Don't worry. It won't be
long. Are you nervous?"
"A little."
"It will be fine. Just tell the truth."
"What will happen to us?"
"I can't tell you that. But don't worry. You will be safe. And
your sister."

The door opened and Shakespeare stood sideways in the
doorway, still continuing a conversation with a member of his
team at a desk nearby. Standing in the far corner of the room

awaiting Shakespeare's call, Jamil glanced across the room. What he saw rocked him to the core, the sight of Sofiya, unaware of his presence, seated in the inner room.

"My God, it can't be," he thought. "Not her!"

But his eyes told him that it was.

"How the hell did this happen? What the fuck is she doing here?"

He remembered the missed calls from Sadie that he should have returned. She must have known. She would have warned him. But it must be her fault that the girl was free. His companion chastised him.

"You trusted a woman, Jamil. Now you're paying the price." Thinking quickly and playing for time, he excused himself on the pretext of needing the toilet, hurrying back out into the corridor and heading for the cloakroom he had passed on the way in. Locking himself in a cubicle, he leaned back against the door, breathing hard. Using his second mobile he rang Sadie's number but there was no reply.

Making his way back to the main office, he rang his official mobile from his second 'phone which he stuffed back into his pocket. Entering the room, he conducted an imaginary conversation with a third party within the earshot of all, taking care not to be in sight of Sofiya. He turned his back as if attempting to make the conversation private.

"But I'm working. I can't come now."

He paused. Shakespeare looked at him expectantly from the interview room doorway.

"Alright, alright. I'll come," he said loudly and cleared the call. Turning back to face the detective, he made his excuses.

"I'm really sorry," he said. "I''ve been called away urgently. I'll ring my boss and ask him to send someone else."

Shakespeare sighed but accepted without argument. In the corridor Jamil called Len.

"I'm really sorry, sir," he began. "But I'm needed urgently at home. It's my wife. Can you send someone else here?"

"Have you started the interview yet?"

"No, sir."

"Right. Go then. I'll see to it. Just go. I'll speak to DCI Shakespeare."

With a sigh of relief, Jamil left the building and made his way to the bolt hole of home to think his way through.

******

DCI Shakespeare entered the interview room with Mickey Gray by his side. He introduced them both to Sofiya and the questioning began. With few answers to give and understanding Ana's intent, Sofiya opted for the truth. It was apparent to her that the point at which the police became more attentive was her account of their arrival in the country. When her narrative reached her rape in the brothel, their questioning became intense.

"This man you say raped you; are you sure it was the same man who came to the place you were taken to when you first arrived? This factory place you described."

"Yes."

"Do you know his name?"

Sofiya shook her head.

"He not tell me. But I hear someone call him something. I not remember......"

"Think carefully. What did it sound like?"

"I think it ..... "

Sofiya paused, then curled her lips to make a 'ch' sound, then 'sh', then 'j'.

"I think it that,"she said, and repeated 'j'.

"Jim, John, Jack?"

She shook her head.

"More," she said. She turned to speak to the interpreter.

"A longer name," the interpreter told them.

"Are you quite sure of this? Are you sure you have not seen someone like him or seen him somewhere before?"

"It him. I am sure; same man. I not forget that man. But you not believe me. I knew you not believe me."

"I didn't say that. I think we'll take a break here. Mickey, it's warm in here. Can you organise some liquid refreshment?"

"Yes, sir."

Suspending the interview, Shakespeare left the room.

Sofiya was in a panic.

"They in it together, the police, that man" Sofiya insisted.

"They send me back to that place. I need get away."

"Look, just calm down. They can't do that. I'm a witness to everything that happens here. Do you trust me, Sofiya?"

The girl thought for a moment. She studied the interpreter who met her gaze calmly, then with little choice to do otherwise, Sofiya nodded.

"Then tell the police everything you know."

"But they not believe me. They say I lie. Say we bad girls. They all in it. Police bad people."

"No, Sofiya. Not here. Just calm down and it will be fine."

"What they do with me? With my sister?"

"I can't tell you that. But you are safe. Just be calm and tell them what they need to know to catch this man."

Len Hutton listened carefully to what Shakespeare was telling him.

"Do you think she's telling the truth?"

"I do. There are two things here. There's your end of things – the trafficking; then there's ours - the rape. She heard someone call her rapist by name but she can't actually remember the name, only that she thinks it began with 'J' or a similar sound. Is someone coming to sit in on the interview?"

Len was thoughtful. The seriousness of how things were progressing, the implications to the department, were of considerable concern.

"I have no-one free right now, otherwise they would be with you already. Anyway, I think under the circumstances it's best that I come myself."

"Good. I agree. I'll wait 'till you get here before I restart the interview."

By the time Len Hutton arrived, Sofiya had calmed down and was willing to give them the benefit of the doubt.

"Perhaps they not in it together," she thought. This new man looked honest. He was older; he looked tired but not unkind, not threatening like that man had been. Perhaps she could dare to trust him. With all comfortably seated and the tape running, the interview was resumed.

"Right, Sofiya. Now tell us again. When you arrived in the country you were taken to this warehouse sort of place. Is that correct?"

"Yes."

"Tell us again who was there."

"There is driver," she began. "And three people wait. Two woman, a man. Then this other man arrive. New man."

"You heard someone call him by his name?"

"Yes."

"Can you remember that name?"

Sofiya shook her head.

"But you think it began with ?" He made the sound.

"Yes."

"What happened after that?"

"This woman take us to a place. Smart. How you say ..?" and again the interpreter.

"Posh," came the explanation with a smile. "It was like – you know, where they do hair. And," she indicated her nails.

"Like a beauty parlour."

The interpreter translated and Sofiya nodded.

"She took us in … "

She referred to the interpreter again.

"in minibus," she continued. "She make me get out. And another girl. We go inside with this girl Sapphire. Only inside I see my sister not with us. The woman is gone and taken my sister with her."

"Do you know the woman's name?"

"The girl Sapphire call her Sadie. And when she come later, she say her name is Sadie."

The officers exchanged enquiring glances.

"Tell us about when you say this man raped you."

Sofiya related the events of the night that still haunted her.

"It was him. 'J'," she concluded.

"How can you be so sure? Perhaps it was someone like him."

Sofiya shook her head emphatically.

"Describe him to us."

The interpreter translated. Sofiya thought carefully.

"High," she said.

"You mean tall?"

Sofiya nodded and turned to consult the interpreter.

"Dark," she continued, "dark skin and hair."

"Glasses?" he indicated with his hands around his eyes.

"No."

"How old?"

Again the interpreter.

Sofiya shrugged.

"Young, old?" Shakespeare prompted.

"Not old. Not boy."

"Anything else you can tell us? About the way he looked."

"Cold. Cold eyes," and Sofiya's resolve weakened. She let out a sob and struggled for composure.

"What these people think," she spluttered. "That because we poor we have no feelings. We just like … what, puppets they can do what they want. They pull strings. Like dolls to play with and treat as they choose?"

The tears came freely.

"Ok, we'll take another break here," and once more, Shakespeare paused the interview and the three men left the room.

In his office Shakespeare spoke with Len and Mickey.

"You're the local boy, Mickey. I need your input here. This Sadie. Do we know of her?"

"We do. Sadie Stanford, sir. Runs a strip club in Soho. East End girl. She was married once but her husband was killed in an industrial accident. He was in construction, I believe. Went to work one day and never came home. I think she was alright until then but it changed her. She used her compensation to buy the strip club and it seems to have been all downhill since then. A real hard piece now. Bitter and twisted. Lots of iffy things over the years. You know, lots of Chinese whispers. Possibly under age girls, some foreign, maybe illegal. But never anything solid; never any proof. They always seemed to disappear from sight the minute we wanted to check them out and everyone else would be legit so we've never been able to make anything stick. She always seemed to be one step ahead."

"Well, she would be, wouldn't she? If she had an ear in immigration. And even in the force for all we know. We need to look out for that."

"I suppose we must."

"She's overdue then, isn't she? Let's see if we can make it stick this time. Be careful who you talk to about the case in the office. We can't take any chances. Take this Sofiya to the club – just outside, I mean. See if she identifies it. But not a word to anyone"

He turned to Len Hutton.

"What do you think, Len? Any ideas who this 'J' might be?"

"I do have someone in mind. Jacob Adama, second generation Afro-Caribbean. Family originally came over on the Windrush. Mother white British national. No record of criminality in the family. We're keeping an eye on him at the moment."

"Well, maybe we should take over that duty. We'd be impartial. Shall I set that up?"

Len nodded.

"Ok, give me the details and I'll get onto it. Mickey, who have we got free to put on this one?"

Arrangements were concluded and Len rose to leave.

"Right, sir. What next?" Mickey asked.

"Well, we'll have to get these two girls into a detention centre or the like. Somewhere safe for the time being. They'll be key witnesses when all this goes to trial."

"You're confident, then?"

"Determined, Sergeant Determined!"

******

Interrogating Ross's computer the officers scrolled through the endless stream of emails in his mailbox and the story that was unfolding had them hooked.

"Looks like he's been trading in illegals for domestic and sex slaves. Look, some of the emails have photo attachments. This girl can only be about 14 or 15 years old. It's going to take a lot of work and a whole team to track down these addresses and recover these people."

"Poor devils. They probably paid a small fortune to get into the country – for this. Worse than they left at home, I'll bet. It's sickening. But at least we have the chance to get them back. If he hadn't been killed in that crash .... "

"Hang on. Look. This one. The photo attached. It's the same woman whose photo was found in his car. Who's it from?"

"An azad@paleblue.com It's a start. Better check him out."

******

Leaving the office at lunchtime, Jacob took his mobile from his pocket as soon as he reached the street. He made a call.

"Hi. It's me. Is the coast clear?"

"Yes."

"I'm on my way."

He hailed a cab and gave the driver an address in Dulwich.

Paying off the cabbie, he glanced over his shoulder, then knocked on the door. It opened as if of its own accord and he disappeared inside with haste. Some two hours later, he re-emerged and, watched by his shadow, hailed another cab. Alighting back at the office, he paid off the cabbie and returned to his post. His shadow logged the time.

******

In the quiet of late evening, Len returned to the offices and by agreed appointment with DCI Shakespeare and night security, keys at the ready, went to Jacob's desk. In their presence, he searched the desk which they found to be unlocked.
Discovering the envelope of money in the bottom drawer, it was agreed. Jacob would be helping with their enquiries in the morning. Shakespeare brought Len Hutton up to date.
"He's been on surveillance today and went at lunchtime to an address in Dulwich. He stayed for over an hour and then returned here to the office. The house is the home of a Mr and Mrs Goss. Apart from that, nothing more to report."
Len gasped.
"Steve Goss. He's another of my officers. I suppose that means they could both be involved. My God. It gets worse."
He shook his head in disbelief.
"Steve's a bit of a maverick, a bit of a stirrer in the department but I'd never have put him down as dishonest. And as for Jacob, I'd have staked my life on his honesty."
"I understand. It can come as a shock to find one of your own has betrayed the rest of the team; everything you stand for. But let's not get ahead of ourselves. I agree it looks suspicious but we could be barking up the wrong tree. I find it strange that this Adama didn't lock his desk knowing this money was here. It doesn't suggest anything sinister. This money could be from something else and he and Goss could just be friends. If it fits with your diary, I'll be here at 9 am in the morning to interview Adama and I'll set up an identity parade to take place at the same time as well."

With a sigh, Len agreed. Leaving with a heavy heart, he set off for home.

Chapter Ten

Tuesday, 16th September

His companion was whispering to Jamil as he entered Len's office, dropping sly words of suggestion into his ear.

"Tell him she's gone. It will make sense after yesterday. And if anyone comes looking .... "

Reading a document, Len looked up only briefly when he heard Jamil's arrival. He continued with his reading, making annotations in the margin of the document.

"Sir, may I have a word," Jamil began.

Len sat back in his seat and put his pen down on the desk. He was in ill humour.

"What is it, Jamil?"

"I'm sorry about yesterday, sir. It was an emergency."

"So you said. What's the problem?"

Jamil feigned a pained expression.

"It's Katya. She's left me. Me and Hasan."

Len was astounded.

"That doesn't sound like Katya. What's brought this on?"

Jamil continued as if in distress.

"It's been going wrong for some time," he began. "It's my fault. She never really wanted a baby. I pushed her into it." He paused, shrugging his shoulders.

"I'm very sorry to hear that. I thought you and Katya were sound. So where's Hasan now?"

"He's with a neighbour. She's a child minder so it's ok for now but I'm going to have to find him a nursery long-term."

"Well, if you need any more time, let me know. But you have to understand I can't let it disrupt the running of the department. You need to get your childcare arrangements sorted as soon as. And where's Katya?"

"I don't know. She wouldn't tell me where she was going. Just said she would be staying with a friend until she'd decided what to do. She might even go back to Turkey."

"Ok. Keep me informed. In the meantime, there have been developments on the insider investigation. The police are due any time to interview Jacob, but keep that to yourself."

"Sir. Will you want me to sit in?"

"I don't think so, Jamil. We'll let the police handle it in their own way."

As agreed, Shakespeare and Gray arrived at Len's office promptly at 9. They discussed the latest developments. Shakespeare began.

"There was an incident last night involving Jacob Adama and Steve Goss."

"Oh?"

"About 9 pm Goss arrived at Adama's flat. There was an altercation at the door with Goss shouting and gesticulating. He then punched Adama and pushed him up against the wall. It looked like he was making some kind of threat. My officers were considering intervening but then after a few moments, Goss left."

"Two villains falling out, do you think?"

"Well, maybe we're about to find out. Have you spoken to Adama this morning?"

"No. In fact, I've deliberately not approached him at all."

"Ok. Well, better call him in then."

Jacob adjusted the knot of his tie nervously. The left side of his face was bruised and swollen.

"Damn," thought Shakespeare. "That could affect the identity parade."

"Sit down, Jacob. This is DCI Shakespeare and DS Gray. They're here to ask you some questions."

Jacob complied. He looked puzzled.

"You were seen having an altercation last night with your colleague, Steve Goss. What was that about?"

The expression of shock on Jacob's face intensified as he realised he had been under surveillance. But why? He was silent, unsure of how to proceed.

"What's your involvement with Steve Goss?"

"He's a colleague."

"Is that all? Just a colleague. Or are you also friends?"

"No. Just colleagues."

Shakespeare tried another tack. He placed a photo of Sofiya in front of Jacob.

"Do you know this woman?"

"No, sir."

"Are you saying you've never seen her, met her?"

"Yes."

"Are you quite certain about that?"

"Yes, sir."

Shakespeare produced the envelope of money.

"This envelope contains £!000. in £10. bank notes. It was found in your desk. Can you tell us where it has come from? How you obtained it?"

Jacob was stunned.

"When? Who found it?"

"Your desk was searched in my presence with Mr Hutton here in attendance."

"I've never seen it before. It isn't mine, sir. I don't know where it's come from. Honest to God, I've never seen it before."

"Well, we'll be checking for fingerprints so you might as well tell us now."

"I swear. I've never seen it before."

His hands moved nervously in his lap and he sweated with tension.

Shakespeare waited, allowing Jacob time to continue but he said no more.

"I'll ask you again. What's your involvement with Steve Goss?"

Jacob sighed, weighing up his options, then spoke quietly.

"I have no involvement with Steve apart from his being my colleague. My involvement is with his wife."

His embarrassment was evident.

"We've been having an affair. That's what the row was about. Somehow Steve found out. She wants to leave him but she can't at the moment because of the boy. Their son. I live in a one bed rented flat. She can't leave until I've put together some money for a bigger ..."

His voice trailed off, his face flushing with panic.

"So that's why you needed this money."

"I know how it looks but I swear, I've never seen that money before. Why are you asking me these questions? What are you accusing me of?"

"We believe someone has been assisting the trafficking of illegal immigrants."

The shock on Jacob's face was convincing and his voice shook with emotion.

"Me? You suspect me?"

The officers waited, allowing the silence to work on Jacob but he remained silent. After consideration for a moment, Shakespeare suspended the interview and stepped outside with Len and Mickey.

"Let's get him to the station and do the ID parade. Then we'll know how to proceed. If it's simply a domestic I don't want to get diverted. But we'll check out his home and his bank statements just to be sure."

"Does that mean you believe him then, sir?"

"I think I do. He doesn't come across as a practised villain. Doesn't have the guile, if you ask me. What about you, Len?"

"I've always thought Jacob to be an honest officer of integrity. I'll be more than disappointed if I'm proved wrong."

Shakespeare nodded.

"Well, let's see if the girl ID's him; that could be the decider on how we proceed."

Len agreed.

As they accompanied Jacob out of the office, he stopped outside the cloakroom.

"I need the toilet."

"I'll wait here," Shakespeare told him. He and Len stood aside talking. Seeing them all leave the main office, Jamil followed and while the two men were turned away from him he slipped quiet and unseen through the door into the cloakroom. Jacob was at the washbasin, splattering cold water on his florid cheeks.

"You alright, Jacob? You look a bit flustered."

Jacob shook his head.

"They think I've been involved in trafficking. Say they found all this money in my desk. I've never seen it before, Jamil. I swear to God I don't know how it got there. But they're convinced it's mine. They're taking me in for questioning."

"Well, can't you invent a story then? Say you won it on the dogs or the horses. Or it's a loan from someone?"

"Such as who. They're gonna check whatever I tell them. And I don't have a clue about horse racing or the dogs. They'd soon work out that I'm lying and that would make things look even worse. I don't know what I'm going to do."

"Well, I'm sorry, Jacob. I can't help you then. You'll just have to convince them they're wrong. Good luck with that. If you need someone to talk to, you know where I am; if I can help in any way."

"Thanks, Jamil. Thanks."

Jamil watched Jacob dab his face dry, then leave, an air of dejection about him.

"He'll never do that," the companion chortled. "He's a loser. Doesn't have the inventiveness to get himself out of it. He's almost hung himself already."

******

At the station, Sofiya paced nervously along the line of men before her. But her response was definite.

"No," she said. "He not here."

"You're sure?"

She nodded.

"I not forget him. He not here."

Shakespeare sighed. He spoke directly to the interpreter.

"Ask her if there's anything more she can tell us. Did the man have any identifying marks, a tattoo, for instance."

Sofiya shook her head.

"No tattoo," the interpreter informed him.

Suddenly Sofiya grabbed the interpreter's arm, her face animated and speaking urgently in Romanian.

"She says he has a scar."

"Where?"

Sofiya raised her hand to the left side of her neck, just below her ear.

"Here," she said. "It here."

Len gasped.

"Oh, my God."

For him the pieces fell rapidly into place. Shooting Len a glance, Shakespeare continued.

"Tell her thank you, she can leave now," He turned to Len.

Len gasped again, "Oh my God."

"What is it?"

"It isn't 'J' for Jacob," explained Len. "It's 'J' for Jamil. Jamil Hussein, my Deputy. It was Jamil who suggested Jacob as a suspect. He could have planted that money without any problem. And he has an old scar, just where she showed us. We've been pursuing the wrong J. Why didn't she tell us this before?"

"Why didn't we ask the question before? Is Jamil in the office right now?"

"He is but he'll be leaving soon on business."

"Mickey, get on to it. I'll organise back-up."

Shakespeare reorganised his team in haste.

******

From the office Jamil took the underground to the lock up to pick up his car, followed discreetly by Sergeant Gray. As they emerged into weak afternoon sunshine, Mickey called DC Ashwood, his partner for the task.

"We've just come out of the tube station. Where are you?"

"South side of London Bridge. I'll head towards you, then. Where are you heading now?"

"Walking down Duke Street."

"I'll get towards you as quick as I can."

"Hang on. He's turning down a side-street."

He paused and held back as Jamil turned into a driveway.

"There's two rows of lock-up garages. I'm just hanging back so he doesn't see me but I can see he's got a bunch of keys out of his pocket. He's opening one of the lock-ups."

Sergeant Gray paused again.

"Ash, how far away are you?"

"Still a few minutes yet. Why?"

"He's backing a car out. 13 plate Mercedes. Gold colour. Unless you can get here quickly we're going to lose him."

"That's a pretty fancy car on his salary, isn't it? 40 odd grand of motor. I can't get to you any quicker. The traffic's heavy, holding me up."

"He's moving off. Nothing I can do. There's no taxi around so I can't follow him. I'll ring the reg number into the office. Maybe they can pick him up on CCTV. Just come and pick me up and I'll talk to Shakespeare about our next move. Check what he wants us to do next."

The instructions from Shakespeare were much as he had expected.

"Right, you wait there for a while until he comes back to the lock-up, then follow him where he goes next. It's dropping dark now so it's probably going to be home. Then get off home yourself but make sure you write up your notes. I'll have someone put on his home address for the night."

Sergeant Gray sighed. He was tired and it was dropping chilly. It had been a long and in some ways boring day but his empty studio was an uninviting prospect, a take-away in front of the tv. He still missed family life, a hot tasty supper waiting, the bedtime story for Amelia, or Millie as he called her. He dismissed the nostalgia and centred on his task. He wanted to see this through, to nail this guy for the crimes they were now certain the man had committed. He resigned himself to the wait.

It was some two hours later by the time Jamil returned after his visit to Hasan. He parked the Mercedes back in the lock-up and padlocked the door, then set off on foot for home. Sliding out of the car, Sergeant Gray left his partner to drive away as he fell into step behind his quarry. Jamil walked briskly. In the lighter traffic and pedestrian activity, he was not so easy to follow and Mickey ducked sideways several times to avoid being seen. Jamil picked up a take-away on the way before letting himself into his own front door. Stepping back into the shadows, Mickey watched Jamil go inside his front door. A car ahead of him briefly flashed its headlights. Peering to recognise its driver in the deepening gloom, he headed for the the unmarked car.

"OK, Mickey. I'm on it for the night. Shakespeare said you can get off home once the man was safely indoors."

"Ok. I'll leave it with you then. Hope you have a quiet night. I'll see you for debrief in the morning."

******

Jamil ate his take-away in ill humour. Without Hasan in the house it felt even emptier. A thin film of dust had settled across the furniture and laminate flooring, scuffs marks and puffs of fluff dotted the rugs and carpets. It rankled him to even think of doing housework. He was a man, it was not a man's job to go round the place with a duster and a vacuum, and the noise of the vacuum cleaner was an irritation. It had always been done while he was not at home. To bring Mina here was far too risky; she could be seen and she would know too much about him. He must get a cleaner - and soon. And he would put the house on the market and move to an apartment. Katya's name was not on the property which he had bought before their marriage.

"Good thing we kept it that way," his companion congratulated him. His mind was made up. He was free now to do whatever he chose. His pay-as-you-go mobile buzzed and he recognised the caller. A voice in Turkish addressed him.

"'Allo."

"Jamil. What's happening? I have people here asking, 'when can I go'? What do I tell them? I am losing money and these people will go to someone else."

"Not yet. I have too much to do at the moment to set things up. Give me a few more days."

"OK. But no longer, or *I* have to find another way. Someone else – understand?"

Jamil sighed.

"It's no good being impatient. We have to be safe or we will just get caught and that will be the end of it all. Just tell people they must be patient if they want to be safe. I'll get back to you soon."

He killed the call with annoyance. He had still been unable to destroy the manifest and Len seemed to be keeping him on a tight lead right now. He felt uncomfortable and frustrated, stuck in the office all day with his movements so restricted. These people pushing for another consignment did not understand these difficulties in their impatience. His companion consoled him.

"They are greedy, these people. Only thinking of their own agenda. They don't care that they could put the whole operation at risk, and your career."

"It's true," he agreed. "It is true. They are fools."

His mood deepened, irascible, petulant and he cracked open a can of beer and gulped down the honey liquid. After several more cans of beer, he fell into bed in a deep sleep.

******

Around Katya's hospital bed the monitors bleeped and spiked a steady rhythm. She lay motionless and silent, a nurse checking her vital signs and WPC Micha Holly sitting at her bedside.
"No change, nurse?"
The nurse shook her head to the doctor who had entered the room.
"Nothing, doctor."
"Have your colleagues been yet?" he asked the WPC.
"Not yet. I'm expecting them any minute. They were sending someone yesterday but they were waylaid by some sort of incident and never made it."
"Well, the sooner we can identify her, the better. The x-ray has shown us no specific damage to the brain but you never know. We can't be sure she won't suffer some minor damage, possibly memory loss or some loss of sensation. There's no reason why she shouldn't regain consciousness fairly soon and the presence of a family member would help to bring her round. Someone familiar to talk to her. Let me know if there's any development."
About to leave the side room, he was met by Shakespeare just arriving.
"Ah, good. I was just asking about you. Any news yet on her identity?" he asked.
Shakespeare shook his head.
"We're circulating her 'photo so hopefully someone will come forward soon. No change in her condition?"
Micha Holly replied.
"No, sir. No sign of consciousness yet."
"I want to know the minute she wakes, right?"
"Yes, sir."
"I'll wait for your call," and with one last glance at the unconscious patient, he left.
"Come on, lady," Micha Holly whispered. "Wake up and tell us your secrets. The world is anxious to know."

******

For a second night Len waited in the deserted office with
Shakespeare and the duty security officer armed with master
keys. Together they tried them one by one until the lock on
Jamil's desk surrendered with a click. Dismissing the security
officer with a promise to return the keys as they left, Len rifled
through the papers in the desk. Discovering the second
manifest, he studied it with interest.

"Another copy. Why?"

They took it to his office to compare with the one in the tray on
his desk and took no time in discovering the difference.

"So that's the way of it. Look, Ben. He's doctored my copy.
There was another lorry."

"The one your duty officer stopped must have been a decoy.
That was Hussein, right?"

Len nodded.

"Well, we're onto it now. First thing in the morning, I will
check this one out myself. This looks like an organised
trafficking ring. Could have been going on for some time."

Len sat in his chair dejected. He took a bottle of whisky and
two glasses from the drawer of his desk.

"Join me?"

Shakespeare nodded, taking a seat to the side. Len spoke with
feeling as the liquid warmed his belly.

"You know, when Jamil joined the service, I was Deputy then.
He hadn't been in the country that long. I took him under my
wing, so to speak. I've supported him through each promotion,
acted as a referee for his first mortgage application. I was even
a witness at his wedding. He has no family in the country so I
stepped into the breach. He came to my home and my wife
cooked him supper. I thought him a decent man; a man of
integrity and justice. We both did, my wife and I. A man with
the same values as myself. To learn how wrong you've been is
a blow. Such a betrayal of trust. But more than that; it's

personal. It's a bitter pill to swallow. But deep down I know now that it's him. I was never quite sold on Jacob, but Jamil; yes, my gut is telling me it's right. Why didn't I see it before?" He took a gulp of the whisky.

"I'm sure you know,"Len continued, "that our borders leak like a sieve. We do the best we can with the resources we have; always undermanned, cuts to the budget. But to find one of your own has betrayed you....."

He shook his head despondently. Shakespeare nodded his understanding.

"But I guess I'm lucky in a sense. In all my career this is the first time it's happened to me. The first bad apple I've ever had in my team or amongst my colleagues."

"It's an experience I hope I'll never encounter," confided Shakespeare.

"And Jacob Adama and Steve Goss?" Len asked.

"I've no reason to believe they're involved at all. Seems to me that this Hussein has set Adama up. We were swayed by his suggestion of Adama so we didn't look further until now. The domestic situation between Adama and Goss is an internal disciplinary matter for you to deal with. I'll concentrate my team now on Hussein."

Returning the keys to the security office, eliciting another promise of confidentiality, the men left, each for their own destination.

******

In the kitchen at the Hutton household, Jessica Hutton spoke to her mother.

"Mum, where's Dad? He promised to help sort out my laptop for me."

Miranda Hutton replied to her daughter.

"He's upstairs. Talking to Peter, I expect. I'm sure he'll be down soon."

Jessica gave a gentle moan.

"Oh, Mum. I really need it for my course work. It's got

to be in by tomorrow.

"Well, you should have done it earlier, then, shouldn't
you, young lady?"

Miranda defended her husband.

"Look, love. You know how it goes. When he has something
difficult to deal with he always talks to Peter. He needs that
this evening. He's had a bad day. Just be patient. He'll be
down soon. Can't you start by hand writing it? Then you can
type it up later."

Peter Hutton had been their only son before his death 18
months before. It had been a slow descent from a normal
healthy teenager to his deathbed. By then the cancer had taken
its toll. Although the conclusion had been expected, the grief
and sense of loss were still raw.

"You think you're prepared, don't you?" Len had confided to
his wife the day that Peter died. "But you're not really. No
matter how much you tell yourself it's better for him, that his
suffering is over, that he's at peace, it's still a shock. It still
hurts like hell when it actually happens."

"Yes, darling. I know. I feel that too. We were still hoping for
that miracle, even though we knew deep down that it wasn't
going to happen. The mind just doesn't want to accept what is
happening; saying no, not yet, not yet. No. He can still get
better. It can still turn out right."

Together they had cried and comforted one another.

It was Len's habit when he was were troubled to talk things
over with his son, sitting on the bed in Peter's room, his hands
resting on the school rugby scarf draped across his lap. It
helped him to indulge his sense of loss and brought him a sense
of calm. And today had been a troubled day. Miranda
respected his need, his way of coping, as indeed he respected
hers.

Journey into Darkness

Chapter Eleven

Wednesday, 17th September

Wiping the sleep from her eyes, Helen answered her mobile, squinting at the bedside clock in the dimness of the half-broken morning light. The alarm had not yet gone off so she knew it must be early.

"Hello."

"Sorry, Helen. I've woken you. I can tell by your voice."

"Martin! Yes, I was asleep. It's really early."

"Well, I didn't know what time you started work and I needed to catch you before you left."

"What is it? Have you found out something?"

"I don't know, Helen, that's for you to tell me. I'm on nights this week. We had a 'photo come in last night appealing for information about a young woman in St Thomas'. She's been unconscious since she was brought in on Sunday. She fits your description of Katya Hussein. I can email it to you if you like."

Helen sat up quickly, scrambling from the bed. She shivered in the morning chill and grabbing her dressing gown from the hook on the door, she tripped her way down the stairs.

"Yes. Can you do it now?"

"I can. Stay on the 'phone while I send it over."

Helen fired up her laptop and waited, her heart thudding loudly, her blood pressure rising. Martin's email fell into her mailbox with a ping. She opened it and opened the attachment, giving a gasp as the pixels fused into an image before her eyes.

"Yes. It's her. It's Katya."

"Helen, I need you to come to the station."

"No problem. I'll come right away."

DCI Shakespeare indicated a seat.

"Helen, thank you for coming in. Please tell me everything you know about this woman."

The words tumbled from Helen's lips in a torrent and she

listened to the story of Katya's discovery with concern.

"It's him – Jamil," she said. "It must be. He's done this to her. Will she be alright?"

"We don't know yet. The doctors feel she should regain consciousness but until then they won't know whether there will be any lasting damage."

"But where is Hasan?"

"A good question. Now we know who she is and her background, we can start to investigate the matter. We'll keep you informed, if that's alright with you. You seem to be more than just her health visitor."

Helen nodded.

"Yes, do. I've been worried about her for some time. We've become friends and I think I'm the only person she has in the world to turn to other than Jamil. Anything I can do to help, anything I can tell you, please let me know."

"Right. We'll be in touch. Thanks again for coming in. Good work, Martin."

Shakespeare imagined the necessary call to Len Hutton, the impact of delivering yet another blow to a man reeling already. It had to be done – and quickly. He reached for the phone.

Martin accompanied Helen to the door.

"Thanks, Martin. I'm so relieved that she's been found. Is it ok if I visit her in hospital?"

"Of course. A familiar voice might help to bring her round. I'll pop in myself at some point."

"Good. Well, I must get off to work now."

Helen turned to leave, then paused.

"Oh, Martin, did you speak to Jules? About our conversation on Saturday? Are you ok now?"

Martin nodded.

"Well, yes, we talked. But no; we're not ok. Jules and I are splitting up, Helen. We've realised that we just want different things from life."

"Oh, Martin. I'm so sorry."

"Actually, Helen, it's a relief. I feel we've been living a lie for so long I'm glad it's out in the open. The elephant isn't in the room any more."

******

The assembled company regarded the photographs on the white board as Shakespeare commenced the morning briefing.
"Jamil Hussein," he began, pointing to the display. "Officer with the Border Agency now under investigation for trafficking."
"Drugs, sir? People?"
"People."
He paused.
"Katya Hussein, Jamil's wife," he continued, moving on. "Found unconscious on Sunday morning at a disused warehouse, a bag stuffed with £5k of used notes in the vicinity. She's been identified by a health visitor who has disclosed a history of domestic abuse. WPC Holly is at her bedside to take any information when she regains consciousness.
"What are the chances of that, sir?"
"Unclear at the moment. We have to be guided by the doctors on that. Jamil is not yet aware of his wife's condition or whereabouts. Significantly he has not reported her missing. Or maybe not. He may just think she is visiting somewhere or someone and is ignorant of what's happened. Somehow though I think there's more to it than that."
"Is there anything to suggest he's responsible for what's happened to her?"
"We'll come to that in a moment."
Shakespeare paused, putting his thoughts in order.
"Sofiya and Anastasiya Albescu, sisters illegally in the country from Romania," he continued. "Alleging they were trafficked in by Jamil Hussein and imprisoned in a brothel. Sofiya, the elder sister, also alleges that Jamil drugged and raped her. She

has identified him from a photograph. The girls managed to escape by digging out the lock on a window and climbing down a drainpipe."

"Plucky," was the murmured consensus.

"Very. Next, Ross McKinnon, owner of a print works in Romford who died in a road traffic accident last weekend. Officers investigating the circumstances surrounding his death visited his home and business address in Dartford and discovered a large amount of printed hardcore porn. Interrogating his computer they further discovered evidence of trafficking of illegal immigrants. There was a photograph of Katya Hussein in Ross's car for reasons we're not yet clear. We're trying to establish a link between him and Jamil Hussein. The IT team are working on that as we speak. There seems to be some confusion as to the whereabouts of Ross's father. He's registered as living at the property and enquiries are continuing in that respect."

"Do you think the father's involved in all this?"

"Not yet known. Until we find his whereabouts and circumstances we won't know the answer to that. Which is where you come in, Jack. I want you to look into that. It's been identified that the old man's pension is being paid into the business bank account so as far as the DWP is concerned he's still there at that address. Neighbours say they haven't seen the old man for years. Speak to the officers who made the initial enquiries. Take it from there and bring back from the property any paperwork that needs looking into. We'll get you and Jim on that, Christine. You're good at that."

"Sir."

"Has Hussein been questioned about the circumstances of his wife's condition?"

"Not yet. He's under surveillance on the trafficking enquiries at the moment. Later today Sergeant Gray and I will be paying him a visit at his home to hear his story on that one. He told his boss that his wife had left him, which may or may not be true. Also that his son was being looked after by a neighbour. The matter of concern at the moment is the whereabouts of

Hasan, their baby son. Five months old. But the Health Visitor tells us that the boy's pushchair and his outdoor clothing are still at the house and that Katya Hussein was afraid of leaving her husband. She also says there has been no sign of anyone at the family home and clearly he's not with his mother. So where is he? According to the health visitor Katya Hussein is a diligent mother devoted to her son. She also told us that Katya wouldn't leave Jamil because she was afraid of losing her son, that Jamil would take the boy from her. Finding Hasan is a priority. I'm reluctant to go in too hard until we have some idea of where the baby is. If Hussein has the boy and is responsible for what's happened to his wife and thinks we're on to him, he could skip the country taking the boy with him. Softly, softly catchee monkey on this one. Right, set to it and keep me informed. But remember, no direct action without our say so. If in doubt you speak to myself or Mickey first," he instructed. "Nothing must put finding this baby at risk. That's our first priority."

The team were smelling blood. They swung into action. As the rest of them left, he spoke to Sergeant Gray directly. "Hold on, Mickey. We need to talk."

In Shakespeare' office, the conversation continued, the planning and assignment of duties to progress their enquiries. Producing another photograph he continued.

"This Sadie Stanford, the strip club owner. Now the Romanian girl has identified her strip club from outside as the building where she and her sister were imprisoned - and the alleyway down the side where they escaped - we're ready to pay her a visit. I'm planning a raid this evening but I want no mention of it other than between ourselves. The drivers of the vehicles will be led to the Club at the time with no prior knowledge of the location. This woman has got away with it for too long. As you say she's always seemed prepared for our visits, this time she must have no hint that this is going to happen and I can't take the risk of insider information. The leak may be from someone in Vice but we also have to consider it could be one of ours."

"That's not good, sir; to think that one of our team is on her payroll. Not knowing who you can trust."

"I agree. But it's a possibility. So we need to be prepared. Tell the team to be ready for a briefing late afternoon. But no word of the reason. Just tell them its about the Hussein case. The Trident team will be leading the raid; they're skilled at it. You carry on with the surveillance of Hussein, Mickey. I know it's tedious but I'm not sure who else I can trust."

Shakespeare watched Mickey leave his office. He would stake his life on Mickey's honesty, his commitment to the job. He was trusting him implicitly, just as Len Hutton had trusted Jamil Hussein.

"God help me if I'm wrong," he breathed to himself.

******

After the tedium of the morning and his brief meeting with Len, Jamil was relieved to get out of the office.

"Visit the businesses I have marked and check them out. I think they're worth a closer look," had been the instruction, but Jamil had his own agenda to pursue, unaware of the eyes that were following his every move and logging his every movement.

"He's heading for the tube station again. I'll be in touch when he comes out the other side. Make sure someone's at the lock-up in case he's heading there. I'll meet up with them there if that's the case"

"Will do."

Jamil backed the Mercedes out of the lock-up and headed for Peckham and the first business on Len's list. He parked clear of the entrance, the Mercedes well hidden from their view. Mickey Gray was parked at a vantage point with both the business and the Mercedes in eyesight. Inside Jamil took his time, inspecting documents, posing questions, going through the motions of an inspection with a confused and concerned

CEO. When at last he re-emerged, he drove to the flat in the Docklands to see Hasan. Parking in the allocated space, he let himself into the apartment block.

"That's interesting. So who lives there then?"

Mickey's partner responded.

"Perhaps he's got another woman tucked away, Sarge."

"Well, it has to be a possibility. The eternal triangle. The usual motive for bumping off the wife. And if that's the case, the baby could be in there too. Check the number of that parking space while I ring in."

Mickey relayed the information to the station.

"We think it's Number 6," he concluded as Natalie held up the relevant number of fingers. "Check it out, will you. Oh, and by the way, there's an agent's 'To Let' board outside. Faulkner and Trent Associates. Get someone to give them a call and see what they can find out."

It was an hour before Jamil re-emerged, smiling broadly. His mind was on pleasure as he pulled away. He headed for Soho where he parked the Mercedes in a side-street, then strolled leisurely towards the strip club, hands in pockets, an air of nonchalance about him. As he turned the corner, the sight that greeted him stopped him in his tracks. The thunderous look on Sadie's face told him all he needed to know, ushered into the police van along with some of her girls. Two uniformed officers stood sentinel at the doorway to bar entrance to members of the public and already a box of documents was being loaded into the van by a plain clothes officer. Mickey 'phoned the station.

"Damn it," said Shakespeare. "I'd hoped it would be over before he went there. I wanted to be able to place him actually inside the club. Oh, well. Done now. We have the girls' statements anyway. See where he goes from there."

Shrinking into the background Jamil began to backtrack, almost colliding with Mickey as he headed back towards his car. Guessing his intention, Mickey turned on his heels and stepped up his pace, overtaking Jamil to walk just ahead of him. He reached Natalie and their car in time to follow the Mercedes and headed off in pursuit at a safe distance.

Secreting the Mercedes safely back in the lock-up, Jamil walked home mulling over the events he had witnessed. His brain was churning, his countenance had changed, a darkness of mood painting his features uglier than merely an hour before. Questions crowded his mind, rushing from one to another. Why had he not heard of the raid? Maybe it was drug-related and nothing to do with immigration, but if so, would the police find the two new girls just arrived? Would they query their legitimacy? Were either of them under-age, for he took no interest in vetting such details of new arrivals? If their illegality was discovered, without him present to stage-manage their responses could they implicate him and betray his involvement? Would they recognise him anyway? His hand went to the scar on his neck. Letting himself into the house, he closed the door behind him with relief. At the fore-front of his mind the need for damage limitation was a priority and the need for an exit plan should the need arise. The companion was nagging and arguing inside his head.

"Take your money and go. Lose yourself in Europe. You have another passport. You have money. What's your problem?"
"But Hasan. What about Hasan?"
"Never mind him," a voice urged. "Just save yourself."
"I can't do that. He's my son. This has all been for him. I must take him with me. And what about Mina?"
"It will be easy. Like Meryam. You can do it the same."
Yes, it had been easy with Meryam. He recalled the scene, her surprise at his appearance. It was her favourite place by the river, where she had once told him she went when she wanted to be alone. She was sitting alone, the look on her face telling him that she was contemplating her secret unrequited love, the love she had hinted at to him in a moment of reflection. She would never love again, she had vowed to him; it was far too

painful. She would marry for money.

"So you don't love me," he had thought. "I am just a fool for your amusement."

Jamil's appearance had interrupted her reflection.

"Jamil. What are you doing here? What do you want?"

His face had betrayed his hatred, looking ugly in his anger, not the malleable lapdog she was accustomed to.

"I don't want anything," he had replied. "I won't want anything from you ever again."

Her look of surprise had turned at first to confusion, then to shock as she saw him raise his arm. Fear flashed in her eyes as she realised his intention. She had no time for self-defence. He heard again the crack as the rock split her skull, the splash as her body hit the water. She had been carried way downstream, far from the site of the crime. Time and the weather eroded any clue as to the point of entry, the cause and reason for her death unresolved, since Meryam herself had always taken care to keep their liaison secret and insisted that Jamil do the same.

"I don't want them gossiping about us in the village, Jamil. You know how the gossips are. They take something good and turn it into something sordid."

It had been her excuse and believing her, Jamil had accepted. He remembered the moment of her death clearly.

"But what about the blood?" his companion cautioned. "You must protect yourself."

Meryam's blood had spattered his t-shirt so he had removed it and burned it later in the woods. Slipping easily back into the village bare-chested had raised no eyebrows in the heat of the Turkish summer, hardly something he could repeat in autumnal London.

"A cagoule,"he suggested. It's easy to burn after. Yes, I can do it. It will be easy with Mina. Easier. Because no-one but me knows who she is, even that she's here. She will be just one more unidentified body fished from the river."

There were plenty of deserted, desolate spots along the river banks, free of prying eyes where her disposal would be possible.

"Yes, it will be fine."

His confidence building, he formed a plan in his mind. He would need time to get a passport for Hasan and that would take a day or two. He would need to sell the Mercedes and buy a less recognisable car. A voice argued with the reasoning.

"But wouldn't it be better to wait and see how the land lies, not just panic into flight? Keep your cool, Jamil. Don't let paranoia push you to do things you don't need."

"Maybe," the companion argued back. "But you must be prepared. If you're out of control of the situation, you would be running blind."

His companion was right. He must keep control and now that Katya was out of the way, there was nothing to stop him being prepared. He would set things in motion tomorrow.

He felt suddenly ravenously hungry and fixed himself a sandwich while he considered. It would be prudent, he decided, to arrange the passport for Hasan in the family name on his second passport. He would deposit the money in the safe in the lock-up into his Turkish bank account. He would ring in sick and take the day to put all in place. The prospect of a new future began to excite him; he and Hasan together. He had money, he could buy them a business, somewhere warm and sunny away from this grey country. As Azad Dalman he would be a big man, a man of substance and influence, not just a cog in a government wheel. A man of gravitas. Yes. He liked that word. Gravitas. He touched the scar on his neck. He could have plastic surgery to remove it, maybe even change his appearance a little. Yes, it was exciting and his companion was urging him on. The other voice had been wrong. His life as Azad Dalman was about to begin.

Azad had been a fellow compatriot also newly arrived in the country. He had rented a room in the same house as Jamil in London's bedsit land but unlike Jamil, his only source of income was from petty criminality. He tried to court Jamil as a friend but his offered friendship was not to Jamil's liking.

"Heh, Jamil. You come with me and my friends to the pub tonight, yes? We have a pint or two, yeah?"

Always Jamil would decline.

"Sorry, Azad. I already have arrangements," he would answer with a nod and conspiratorial wink.

"Ah, you old dog, you. Some lady somewhere, huh?"

And Jamil would smile but say nothing. There were always a girl or two around in Jamil's life but nothing serious, nothing he wished to make public. He regarded women only useful for sex, avoiding any public show of commitment.

"Oh, Jamil, can't we go out somewhere? I want us to be seen together."

"Where would you like to go?"

"A restaurant. Somewhere nice."

Frugal as ever, Jamil would take them for a Brick Lane curry, or to an inconspicuous address in backstreet Chinatown until he tired of their company and ended the liaison in a cruel and perfunctory way.

"Jamil, why haven't you called me?"

"I would have thought that was obvious."

The only person to whom he revealed his early liaisons was Azad to excuse himself from Azad's company. He had seen Azad's friends at the front door and the street outside the house. They were uncouth, common types, frequenting a sleazy, twilight kind of landscape. Jamil's ambitions extended beyond their borders.

On one such evening, Jamil was locking his door to leave. The front door of the house was open and the falling evening light streaked into the hallway. From the landing where he stood, Jamil had watched as bodies filled the open doorway, two burly men, one either side of Azad who they were bundling unceremoniously into the street. Azad was protesting, struggling to get free. Something about the men's demeanour was suggestive of violence, about Azad's that demonstrated terror. Jamil had slunk back around the corner of the landing out of sight. He was in no doubt of Azad's fate. The door to Azad's room was open and he stepped inside and peered through the curtains to the street below. The men were bundling Azad into a car, an inconspicuous old Ford that had seen better days. With Azad squeezed between them in the back seat, the car drew away. Jamil looked around the room. It was untidy, grubby, unlike his own which he kept in pristine neatness. On the cabinet beside the bed were Azad's keys and his wallet. He picked up the wallet and looked inside; a few banknotes of little denomination, a bank card and a slip of paper. Opening the paper Jamil found what he thought must be the pin number to Azad's bank account.

"Stupid fool," he thought. The companion had intervened. "That could be useful, Jamil. And he won't be needing it, not where he's going. Maybe he has a passport too."

Rummaging in the drawer of the cabinet, it was easily found. Jamil took the keys, left the room and locked the door.

Azad Dalman was not seen again, his disappearance dismissed by the landlord as the occupational hazard of a tenant skipping without paying his rent. The absence of his wallet and passport were proof positive that he had done a moonlight flit. Replacing Azad's photograph with his own in the passport, Jamil's co-existence as Azad Dalman was under-way.

Now there was much to do in preparation and of one thing he was sure. With thoughts and ideas whirling in his head, tonight would be a sleepless night.

******

Sadie was giving away nothing. With her solicitor beside her, apart from giving her name and address, her response to all questions was 'no comment,' her voice steady and resolute. Outside the door, it was agreed that she remain in custody until they were ready to charge her. Shakespeare was confident. "I reckon we have her this time. I reckon we do."

Journey into Darkness

******

Facing Shakespeare across the table, the duty solicitor beside her, Ebony was apprehensive.

"She looks young, vulnerable," thought Shakespeare. "Unlike the girl Sapphire who is already hard and immersed in the ways of the criminal fraternity. This girl is fragile."

He began gently.

"Ebony. That isn't your real name, is it?"

Ebony was guarded.

"Can you tell me your real name?" he asked softly.

She looked at the solicitor who nodded.

"Lauren."

"Lauren. Nice name. Unusual and very pretty. So – Lauren. May I call you that? How did you come to be working at the Club?"

Again she was guarded but replied flatly.

"I had nowhere else to go."

"Lauren, how old are you?"

Again the solicitor nodded.

"17."

"And how long have you been working at the Club?"

Lauren shrugged but said nothing.

"Did you run away from home?"

A pause, then she said "I might have."

"But you're not listed as a missing person, I think. You must have family, don't you?"

"Just my mother. She's an alcie. Always out of it. She wouldn't care."

Shakespeare paused out of compassion.

"So how long have you been working at the Club, Lauren? A year? Two?"

"Maybe."

From the folder on the table, Shakespeare took out two

photographs and slid them across in front of her.

"Have you ever seen these girls?" he began.

The expression on Lauren's face gave her away. Her eyes widened, her mouth opened as she drew in a silent breath. She was struggling not to panic. What should she say? If Sadie believed she had grassed there would be trouble. Without the Club and Sadie, where would she go? What would she do? She was afraid. She remained silent. Guessing the reason for her hesitation Shakespeare continued.

"There's no need to be afraid, Lauren. No-one is going to harm you. Sadie will not be going back to the Club. She's in custody and she's going down for a long time."

"So what about me? What's going to happen to me?"

"It's ok. You're not being charged with anything. You are just helping us with our enquiries. We can help you get your life back on track if that's what you want. Go back to school maybe, or different work. You can start here by telling us what you know. But you have to start that process yourself. What do you think?"

Tears welled in Lauren's eyes. She longed for freedom but part of her was afraid of it, afraid of the alternative to what was now familiar. She had not forgotten those first few days on the streets. It had not been as she had expected. It had been hard, demeaning, the rummaging for food in bins outside restaurants, drinking from the taps in station cloakrooms where she went to wash and clean her teeth, scraping out her last few pence, an experience she did not want to repeat. Until Frankie had picked her up sleeping rough under the bridge by the station.

Lauren's story.

Life had begun well for Lauren. They had been like any other family, she and her Mum and Dad. She still remembered those happy days, the family outings, her Dad swinging her round and round in the garden to her squeals of delight. But then the bad times had begun. Her Nan on her mother other's side died, the only grandparent she had ever known,. Her mother

indulged her grief in a protracted glut of self- indulgent
drinking that seemingly had no end. There were the rows, her
father's anger as he poured the alcohol down the sink and
tossed the empty bottles into the dustbin to her mother screams
and protests in response.

"You still have a husband. And you have a daughter to care
for. You need to pull yourself together."

"I can't. I've tried but I just can't."

"Then you need help. You're an alcoholic."

"That's not true. I will stop, I promise."

But her promise had been a hollow one.

One day her father had left them. He tried to take Lauren with
him but her mother had held onto her, screaming and crying.
So he had told Lauren he would always love her, that he would
come to see her as often as he could and he had come – for a
while. But then his visits became less and less frequent until he
stopped coming altogether. He had a new family by then, a
new little Lauren to love and care for. And her mother was
sinking more and more into oblivion.

They had still had good times, she and her mother, when her
mother was briefly sober. But those times became fewer as her
mother's sickness deepened, the abuse and neglect becoming
worse. There were no more good times and out of her own
embarrassment, Lauren would never take friends home so
increasingly she had none. Except for Chloe, that was, until
Chloe found herself a boyfriend and had no time left for her
friend.

Lauren's 14th birthday passed little noticed, just a cheap card
from her mother bought from the local corner shop on her way
back from the off-licence.

"I'll buy you something nice when I get my next allowance,"
but the 'something nice' had never appeared. And at school her
grades were falling, her teachers more and more concerned at

the girl's declining demeanour. When Social Services knocked on the door, her mother refused to open it, making Lauren hide with her behind the bedroom door. At 15 years old, the final confrontation came.

Her mother had not been sober for days, lying in an alcohol-induced sweat-drenched stupor. Lauren made snacks for her meals. She washed her own clothing and cleaned the house as best she could. When her mother at last began to emerge from her overindulgence, she berated the girl angrily for no reason at all. It was too much to bear. Lauren packed her bag, took what money she could find in the house – and left.

She hitched a lift to London on a lorry, avoiding the driver's suggestive gaze. She would get herself a job, waiting on tables, cleaning, anything that would pay her enough to eat and find a room. She looked old enough to pass for 16 and was sure she would find something. But it had not been so easy. There were jobs but the pay was not enough for her to live and for every job there were a queue of hopefuls with references and experience she did not have. She was in despair. And then she met Frankie.

"Heh, girl. What's a beautiful girl like you doing here? You should be a model, or somethin'."
At first she had been wary but he had lulled her into trusting him until she confided her situation.
"I've got nowhere else to go," she told him.
"Look, I know this woman. She owns a club an' she's lookin' for a waitress. Some of her girls live in. She might be able to help you. I'll take you there."
"But I need a wash. And my clothes … "
"Yeah, well, you can come to my place. Have a shower and change. Make yourself look really pretty."
So she had put her trust in Frankie. She stayed with him for a few days. He fed her and bought her clothes and a necklace with a little silver heart hanging from it. He placed it around

her neck as they lay in bed together. He had been her first.
"Because you're my girl an' I luv you," he told her.
Then he took her to Sadie. It was easy to begin with.
Waitressing was easy, except by the end of the night her feet
were aching. The room was small but it was hers. And Frankie
came to see her one time. Then things had changed.

"This client," Sadie told her. "He wants to have a drink with
you. In private, upstairs. We have special rooms for clients to
meet with our girls. Just be nice to him, give him what he
wants and there'll be an extra little tip in your pay packet."
And so it had begun. Frankie didn't come to see her again. She
saw him one more time, though; when he brought another girl
to the club. The girl was wearing new clothes and a necklace
around her neck with a little silver heart hanging from it. It had
hurt because now she knew the truth. Frankie had used her,
soiled her and then discarded her like an old and broken toy.
In time, the girl and Lauren had become friends. You can get
used to anything if you have to. So what now if there were no
Club and no Sadie?

******

Shakespeare continued his persuasion.
"We believe these two girls were brought into the country
illegally and held at the Club against their will; that they were
being forced into prostitution. Have you seen them before?"
"Where are they?" she blurted. "Are they alright?"
"Yes, they are safe. They are with us. They have told us
everything. You would only be confirming what we already
know."
In a wave of relief and angst rolled into one, Lauren let go and
unburdened her heart and soul. DCI Shakespeare had
everything he needed to know.
"We have a bed for you at a hostel if you want it. WDC Walsh
will take you there."
Lauren looked down at her salacious clothing. It screamed of

139

her lifestyle.

"Like this? They'll know what I am."

"Lauren, you are a young girl who needs help; that's all. But if it makes you feel better, WDC Walsh will take you back to the Club to shower and change first. You have other clothes there? Jeans and things?"

She nodded.

"Ok? Off you go then."

"You're not charging her, sir?" asked Mickey when she'd left the room.

"No, Sergeant; no charges. She's a victim, just as the Albescu sisters are victims. Even more so in her case. What purpose would it serve to give her a record when with a bit of help and rehabilitation she has the chance to get her life back, to build a good life for herself and become a successful member of society. Surely that has to be a better option. Giving her a record would only put barriers in her way."

He paused, then quoted:

> "The quality of mercy is not strain'd
> It droppeth as the gentle rain from heaven
> upon the place beneath: it is twice blest;
> it blesseth him that gives and him that takes;
> 'Tis the mightiest in the mightiest"

"I like that sentiment, Mickey. Seems to me we could do with a bit more of it in today's world."

"Shakespeare, sir? You're a Shakespeare fan?"

"I'm married to a classical actress and have a son at drama school, Sergeant I was bound to be introduced to my namesake, don't you think? You know any?"

"Only schoolboy stuff, sir. Star crossed lovers and all that. Can't say it did a lot for me. You must get comments all the time, though."

"I do. But at least my parents didn't call me Shylock."

"You're not a descendant, are you? Of him, I mean."

Shakespeare laughed.

"What, of Will the Bard, you mean? Good God no, not that I know of. Just a pretender. So what's your passion, Mickey? What floats your boat? What does it for you when you need to switch off after a really rubbish day."

Mumford and Sons, sir.

"Mumford and Sons! Sorry. I'm not with you. Who or what are Mumford and Sons?"

"They're a band, sir. The best. Seen them several times at festivals. They're my thing."

******

Late in the night, Lauren curled gratefully between the clean, fresh sheets of her hostel bed. A tear slipped unsolicited from her eye, then another, and another, a gentle crying like the drizzle that falls in spring to wash away the winter's grime. Over the following days, with gentle care around her she slept at will, she cried at will, she ate when she was hungry. The tears came and went like April showers. The process of healing had begun. It would take time; much time. But the future she had hoped and dreamed of many months before seemed once again a distant possibility that beckoned her on.

"For every one like you we are able to help back into daylight from the darkness," Shakespeare told her, "there are a hundredfold and more beyond our reach."

Chapter Twelve

Thursday, 18th September – am

Investigations had revealed that No. 6 of the apartment block had recently been let to a Mr. Azad Dalman for an initial period of 6 months. The description of Mr Dalman fitted exactly to that of Jamil Hussein, even down to the scar tissue on his neck beneath the left ear.

"This Mr Dalman paid 6 months rent up front by bank draft drawn on Turkish Bank UK. With fees that's upwards of twelve grand. He used a box number and a smart 'phone for correspondence and gave Turkish Bank UK as a reference. From the description it sounds like he and Jamil are one and the same."

"Right, Mickey. WDC Walsh and DC Hanrahan. I want them both on surveillance of that apartment while you carry on with Hussein. Keep me informed. Oh, and get onto the IT people and tell them to do a search on McKinnon's computer under the name of Azad Dalman."

"Yes, sir."

By mid-morning, diligence was rewarded.

"Heh up, whose this leaving the apartment, then? Do you think that's our party?"

Mina pulled closed the outer door behind herself and baby Hasan tucked snugly into his pushchair. Walking briskly in the direction of a small shopping area ahead, she talked soothingly to a disgruntled baby Hasan chewing on the ear of his blue fluffy rabbit.

"If it is she doesn't look much like an illicit lover, does she? Mousy little thing if that's who we're looking for," observed DC Natalie Walsh.

"You're right there, Nat. Wonder what her purpose is. I can't see it, not with his wife being such a looker."

"Well, I'm just about to find out," and Natalie opened her car door and left. She walked quickly, gaining ground on Mina from behind until, drawing level, she engaged her in conversation.

"Excuse me, I wonder if you can help me. I'm looking for Mitre Street. Do you know where that is, only, stupid of me, I've left my A-Z at home?"

Mina stopped, startled, a little flustered.

"Sorry," she began. "I not live here long. I not understand. Sorry."

She started as if to move forward, but Natalie stepped casually across her path, preventing her from continuing her journey.

"Mitre Street," she repeated. "Do you know where it is?"

She turned her gaze to Hasan.

"Oh, I'm sorry. Your baby is not happy," and she bent to Hasan, speaking to him in a soothing voice. On the subject of Hasan, Mina responded readily.

"No, he not happy. I think it – here," and she indicated her teeth.

"Ah, he's teething. Oh, poor chap. And he's so cute. What's his name?"

"Hasan."

"Oh, poor baby Hasan," and Natalie bent to observe him closely, the olive skin, the dark hair like his father. His grizzle intensified to a yell and she retreated quickly.

"I'm so sorry to have bothered you," she exclaimed. "I can see you need to get on," and she stepped aside for Mina to hurry by. Back in the car, Natalie took no time in ringing Shakespeare.

"I think we've found baby Hasan," she told him.

"Good work, Natalie. Stay with it. I'll be paying a visit as soon as I can."

Shakespeare's office door swung open.

"Sir, IT have been on the 'phone. They've found the connection with our Mr Dalman; an email from Azad attaching the 'photo of Katya Hussein. Mr Azad gives him a mobile number for

contact and McKinnon responds with a 'phone number of his
own."
"Both unregistered, I'll guess?"
"Yes, sir."
"Well, don't try them. We'll save that for when Hussein is
being questioned."

Returning from the pharmacy with the medicine for Hasan,
Mina fed him a spoonful, then gave him his lunch and his
bottle. She changed his nappy and settled him in his cot. Tired
from his grizzly morning, it took no time for him to fall asleep.
Mina watched him lovingly, planted a kiss on his forehead and
left the nursery, gently closing the door. The ring of the door
chimes took her by surprise.

Mina opened the door cautiously with the security chain firmly
in place. She was surprised to see the officers standing in the
hallway. She recognised the woman from earlier.
"Good afternoon, ma'am. Is Mr Dalman available please?"
"Mr Dalman?"
"Yes, Mr. Azad Dalman. He rents this apartment."
"Oh, no. You are at wrong place. Not Mr. Dalman."
"But the agent gave us that name. The agent the flat was rented
though. You say no, not Mr Dalman, so who rents this
apartment then?
"Mr Jamil. This his apartment," Mina blurted.
"Mr Jamil who?"
Mina looked confused. She regretted having given them any
information but now she felt impelled to continue the
conversation. She had never asked Jamil's family name, nor
Hasan's. She paused, then admitted her ignorance.
"I not know."
"He is not your husband?"
"No. I look after baby."
"May we come in, Miss ah?"
Mina's alarm increased. Jamil had counselled her against

talking to strange people. He would be angry with her. Shakespeare produced his police ID and noted the alarm on Mina's face turn to panic.

"Look, miss. There's no need to be alarmed. I think there has been some confusion here. Can you just let us in, please, so we can clear this up?" and Shakespeare indicated to her to open the door. Not knowing what else to do, Mina released the chain on the door and stood aside for the police officers to enter. Shakespeare again indicated for her to go down the hallway and, closing the door behind them, he and Natalie Walsh followed her into the living room. She sat on the sofa, nervous, pale, her head bowed, hands folded tensely in her lap.

"Right, then. Let's be polite, shall we? I'm DCI Shakespeare and this is WDC Walsh. Do you mind telling us your name?"

"Mina."

"Mina …. ?"

"Mina Pavel."

"Ok. And where are you from, Mina? Your country?"

"From Romania."

"Right, Mina. So you tell us a Mr Jamil rents the apartment. What is your relationship to him?"

"I not understand."

"This Mr Jamil. Are you his wife?"

Mina shook her head violently.

"Oh no. No. I just work."

"I see. What work do you do, Mina?"

"I look after his boy. Baby Hasan. And keep apartment."

"And where is Baby Hasan now?"

"In his bed, sleeping," and she pointed towards the nursery. With a nod from Shakespeare, Natalie rose from her seat and left the room to investigate. Shakespeare watched Mina carefully while they waited, gauging her nervousness from the fidgeting of her hands, the tension evident in her body. He guessed she was illegal in the country, no doubt brought in on one of Jamil's little jaunts and now fearful of what was likely to happen to her. Natalie returned, nodding to her boss and

145

reseating herself to continue the conversation.

"So does Mr Jamil live here – in the apartment?"

"No. Only me and baby."

"And where is baby Hasan's mother? Does she live here?"

Mina shook her head vigorously.

"No. She left. He tell me."

"Ok. So when will Mr Jamil be coming?"

Mina shrugged.

"He come every day, to see Hasan."

"Has he been today?"

"No. Maybe after working."

A cry from the nursery gave warning that Hasan was awake. Mina rose quickly, anxious to attend to him before he became distressed. Shakespeare rose, too, a move echoed by his officer.

"Ok, Mina. Not to worry. You see to the baby. And we'll come back to see Mr Jamil later. We'll let ourselves out."

They left a confused and vulnerable Mina, anxiety evident in her face and her demeanour as she wondered now what she was involved in, the opportunity she had thought was in her grasp diminishing like the smoke from a dying bonfire.

Sitting in the car once more, the officers discussed their next move.

"Right, well, it's clearly the baby. I want to be here waiting when Hussein makes an appearance."

Shakespeare's mobile buzzed loudly.

"Get on to Mickey and find out where he is at the moment. I'll just take this call."

They each indulged in conversations on their 'phones until exchanging information.

"Mickey says he's at some firm in Greenwich, sir. Making enquiries, according to his boss. He walked there from his office. No sign of the Mercedes."

"That was WPC Holly at the hospital. Katya Hussein seems to be regaining consciousness. I need to go there but I don't want

146

Hussein to come back here and speak to this Mina. She might have 'phoned him to tell him we've been round but there's nothing we can do about that. He's got another 'phone that we don't have a trace on. You and Hanrahan take this Mina and the baby into the station. I want that baby safely in our care before we pick up Hussein. It's my bet that he'll go to the lock-up first to pick up his car so there should be time. I'll get a taxi to St. Thomas's. Any problem, ring me. Timing couldn't be worse. I'm supposed to be at The Globe for my wife's first night. She's playing in 'Measure for Measure'. I just hope my boy's made it or we'll both be in the doghouse."

******

Hasan's crying was audible from outside the door as WPC Walsh rang the bell. His crying ceased. Peering over the chain through the gap between the door frame and the door, Mina was alarmed to see uniformed police standing in the hallway.
"Hello, Mina."
Mina stared in confusion.
"Would you open the door, please? We need you to come with us to assist with our enquiries. "
"What you mean? Why you back?"
"We'll explain that at the station, miss. Would you just open the door please?"
In her arms, Hasan whimpered. Torn between refusal and assent, she looked down into his fretful face and knew what her option must be. She released the chain and allowed the officers in. As they instructed, she packed his bag with everything necessary for Hasan's comfort.
"Do you have a passport, Mina?"
"No, Mr Jamil have."
When all was ready, she followed them dutifully to the car, outwardly displaying calm and acceptance. But inside she was crying, distraught, fearful of the path ahead. They would send her back where she had come from, back to a home where she had not been wanted, would be even less so now that she had

147

failed. Her money was all gone, stolen by people who had lied to her; her passport was a fake. She knew what her prospects were, nothing but poverty, hardship and rejection. Her life was in tatters. There was no-one now who would help her.

******

On his way to the hospital, Shakespeare's mobile rang again.
"Hello. Shakespeare."
"Sir, it's Mickey."
"Yes, Mickey. What can I do for you?"
"I'm sorry, sir, but I've lost him. I got swamped by a crowd in the underpass by the Cutty Sark. I think he was heading for the DLR but I can't be sure."
"Damn. He could be on his way to the flat and they're just picking up Mina Pavel and the baby. I just hope he doesn't get there before they're safely in the car. I'm just arriving at the hospital. Ring Natalie and warn her."
"Right, sir. I'm really sorry."

******

In the street, Jamil was approaching the apartment walking. He had taken the Mercedes to a dealer with the explanation for its disposal as financial.
"I just can't afford to run it," he told him. "I need something more economic."
Producing the paperwork in the name of Azad Dalman, they had agreed a price and the money transferred to his Turkish bank account. Unconvinced by Jamil's story, the dealer had got himself a good deal. Jamil knew he had been cheated, but it was a compromise he had to swallow. All he needed to do now was buy something less conspicuous elsewhere. He had tried to contact Ross to get a passport made up for Hasan without success. The man was still not answering so he sent a text instead. He was irritated by Ross's silence.
"Come on, you bastard. Get back to me," he muttered as he

neared the apartment block. The sight ahead of him set his
stomach churning. His son in Mina's arms disappeared into a
police car which sped away. He ducked out of sight into the
shadows of the underground car park as they passed him. He
could see Mina in the back seat, Hasan in his baby seat by her
side. Leaning against a pillar, his breathing shallow, his brain
was incoherent in his panic.

"You fool," a voice told him. "You should have listened to me.
You should have run while you had a chance. What now? You
have put us at risk. What now?"

"But what of Hasan?" he spluttered. "What of my son?"

The voice and the companion began to argue once more. He
clasped his hands to his head.

"Stop. Stop," he muttered. "Stop. I can't think right when
you're on at me. I can't think what to do."

******

"Hasan; my son. Where is Hasan?"

At St Thomas's Shakespeare sat patiently at Katya's bedside.
"He is safe, Katya. Quite safe. Don't worry. You'll see him
soon. Just take your time. Tell me what happened to you; you
remember, before your fall at the warehouse."

Katya began her story.

"We were in the kitchen. Saturday morning. It was strange.
Jamil was strange. He was being really nice. He poured me
coffee which I thought was nice of him. Unusual. Usually he
expect me to do everything but this morning he did it for me.
Hasan was in his baby seat for breakfast. I must have fallen
asleep. Next thing I know I am in this awful place."

"Probably Jamil drugged you. The coffee maybe?"

Katya nodded.

"Yes. I guess," she said sadly. "He came to the warehouse
after I had freed myself. I watched him from where I was
hiding."

"We found the rope he'd used to bind you, and the tape he used on your mouth. We've matched the DNA."

Katya looked down at her wrists, the marks from the rope still visible. She touched her mouth, still sore from ripping away the tape. She continued. Her voice was weak but her recollection coherent. She related the events leading up to her fall.

"There was a bag. A bag full of money."

"Yes, we found that, too. We found a partial fingerprint on the handle of the bag."

Katya began to cry.

"How could he hate me so much? What did I do to make him hate me that much?"

Shakespeare leaned forward and took her hand.

"Nothing, Katya. You did nothing. Jamil is a sick man, a bad man. But it's over now."

"Yes, he is a sick man. He has nightmares, you know. He wakes in the night sweating and shaking. I ask him many times when we were first married what it was that caused them. I even suggest he seek help. Counselling, or something. But he wouldn't have it. He would tell me nothing. I wish I could have got through to him, helped him in some way."

"Be careful what you wish for, Katya. Who knows what lies in his past? A twisted personality like this doesn't appear overnight. You may rather not know."

Katya nodded with a sigh.

"Yes, you're right. But it's in my nature, you see, to see the best in people. And there were some good things about him; in the beginning."

"That's why he married you, Katya. He identified that trust and honesty in you, your willingness to always be forgiving whatever he did."

"Well, not this. He has betrayed my trust this time beyond anything I could have imagined. I knew about the woman; or women. I lived with it for Hasan's sake. But I can never forgive this. My grandmother warned me, you know. My Ebe. She saw it in him. I should have listened to her; trusted in her judgement. But he persuaded me she was wrong about him.

He was clever. He never said she was wrong; never showed anger towards her. Just suggested that she was - how do you say? Too protecting of me. Loved me too much to let me go not just to him but to anyone. Like he pitied her."

"Mmm, but it's over now. For you. Time to get your life back."

"Yes. And Hasan. My lovely Hasan. You say you have Hasan safe?"

"We do."

"I need to see him. Please. I must see my baby. I miss him. He will be missing me."

"I'll arrange it. Don't worry."

A nurse intervened.

"I think that's enough. Katya needs some rest now."

******

Returning to the station, Shakespeare found pieces of the jigsaw falling into place thick and fast as information came in, but with each answer came another question. Their enquiries were spreading outwards like the spinning of a spider's web set to trap a fly.

"Sir, we've received a text from Azad Dalman on Ross McKinnon's mobile. Says he needs a passport for his son."

"That makes sense. So he's getting ready to run. That raid at the Club must have really rattled him. Put out an all ports alert in both names and on his vehicle, though If I were him I'd get rid of that car pretty quick. We could check local car dealers to see if he's traded it in for something less noticeable but we don't have much time. If he gets to Europe we've pretty much lost him. He could go anywhere. We need to get onto this promptly."

******

"Sir, we've received an email from the Turkish police. The trace we ran on Azad Dalman in Turkey. They've come back with a crime sheet, a list of mostly petty crimes. But they also sent us his mugshot. Interesting, isn't it?"

A photo was pushed across the desk.

"So. Not Jamil Hussein, then. So how did Jamil steal this Azad's identity? And where is the real Azad Dalman? With every answer we get to our questions on this case there seems to be a host of other questions cropping up to take their place. It's endless. Better check out missing persons and see if this Dalman character has been reported as missing."

******

"Sir, the IT boys have found an email link to a party up north." Another head had appeared around his office door.

"McKinnon had forwarded Katya Hussein's 'photo on. Looks like he was planning to sell her on to someone but as yet they've been unable to identify the other party. They're still working on it to come up with more details."

"How do they do that? Track down people over the internet?"

"Well, sir, it's like a paper trail. They .... "

"Never mind. I don't really want to know. Bores the hell out of me, all that IT stuff. Goes right over the top of my head. But they get results. That's all I want to know. My God. What the hell did these people have planned for this poor woman? If it hadn't been for that accident on the M25.... Keep at it. The net widens."

"When will it ever end," he thought. "All this trafficking; this selling of souls out of greed?"

It was a rhetorical question he posed himself; the answer followed on at a pace. It would never end. There would always be the vulnerable and the unscrupulous ready to exploit them. When the borders were open to some, there would be others to whom the borders remained legally closed. It would never end. He heaved a heavy sigh.

"But we'll catch more than one fly in this web," he promised himself. "Or my name's not Ben Shakespeare."

******

"Looks like a perfectly ordinary house, doesn't it?"

"It does. But you know what they say. Never judge a book by its cover."

Walking up the steps at the address in New Cross that had been the sisters' original destination, officers from the Met and the Border Agency approached the house together and knocked on the door. Their knock was answered by a young man of unidentifiable race. He gasped in surprise at the sight of the officers who stepped forward to pass him into the hallway.

"Hey, what you want, man? You can't come in here."

"We can and we are," came the reply. "We have a warrant to search these premises, Mr .. aah?"

He gave no reply.

At first sight the ground floor appeared no more than an ordinary family home, the décor, the odd personal item of clothing hanging on a chair or a magazine open on the floor. Upstairs was to reveal a different story. In the first bedroom, all appeared normal, a homely place of safety, but in each of the other bedrooms a bowl containing condoms sat in a prominent position and the unkempt beds bore the marks of recent activity. But it was the garden at the rear that held the most devastating secret of all.

Sheltered on either side by high hedging, the garden afforded a privacy from the adjoining properties. Against the one boundary stood a ramshackle wooden shed of large proportions, its door secured with a heavy padlock. Threaded through a gap in the boarding at the end an electric cable stretched across from the fanlight window at the rear of the kitchen swinging frighteningly in the breeze. Cutting the chain across the doorway secured by a padlock the officers prised open the door to peer into the dimly lit interior.

"Oh, my God."

The officers expressed their horror. Eyes peered at them through the gloom, the terrified eyes of five, six young girls and a boy, each seated on a mattress lined against the wall, their meagre belongings scattered around them. The air was damp and musty, the atmosphere clammy from the lack of ventilation. In the centre an old paraffin heater was the only source of warmth and an ancient tv crackled in the corner, the only source of entertainment.

"It's an absolute death trap."

"You're not kidding. One spark from those dodgy electrics and the whole place would go up like a tinder box – and them with it."

"No Health and Safety Officer here then. I'll bet they're not on the minimum wage with an annual leave entitlement. And I wouldn't mind betting there's a fair few of these dotted across the capital."

"Not just the capital, mate. This isn't the first we've come across. They're countrywide. We've already come across several."

"Our kids don't know they're born, do they?"

"You're right there well enough. If mine don't have the latest piece of technology, or the designer trainers, they think they're deprived."

They stopped to discuss their next move.

"I'll ring in to DCI Shakespeare. I suggest you ring in to your boss at the same time. We're going to need back up to take them in. And by the look of them they all need checking over by a doctor."

Replacing the receiver after taking the call, Ben Shakespeare shook his head in despair.

"Like I said - endless."

******

Again the 'phone on Shakespeare's desk shrilled.

"Ben, it's Len Hutton. We've had a call from Jamil this morning. He's called in with an urgent request for leave. The story is a sick relative that he needs to visit in Turkey."

"Damn," thought Shakespeare. "He's definitely on to us then. He really is getting ready to run. We need to move quickly now."

"What did you tell him?" he asked.

"I told him to take whatever time he needed but to keep me informed. Have you found the boy yet?"

"Yes. And Katya Hussein has regained consciousness. She's given us a full account of what happened. He'll be charged with conspiracy to murder as well as the trafficking charges. From what we've learned so far it seems clear he hired someone to do away with her. Quite what the plan was we're not clear but there's no doubt about that much."

Len was shocked even more.

"My god, that as well. I can barely believe it. He clearly has no moral compass whatsoever. What makes people like this, what turns them bad? I never can understand it. Is it their nature or their background? Katya seemed such a lovely girl to us. His story of her leaving Hasan didn't sit well with that but sometimes women do reject their children. Post-natal depression and all that. Just shows, doesn't it? You never really know someone outside of your own, do you?"

"Ah, the old nature versus nurture debate. Can't answer that, I'm afraid. But whatever the reason, there can be no justification for the things he's done."

"No but I'll bet his defence will try. Diminished responsibility or something."

"Well, we'll not let him get away with that one."

"But there's more."

"Oh god, more? What next? Go on; hit me with it."

"Our guys - yours and mine - they've discovered a shedful, literally a shedful, of illegals kept in absolute deprivation. But

155

this came from the Romanian girls - their contact in Romania. I'm not sure Hussein is responsible for this. We've emailed the Romanian police to get onto it their end. Greed, that's all it's about as far as I'm concerned. Pure, unbridled greed."

"Well, whether he is or not, we have to get him, Ben. We have to. And as many of the others as possible."

"Don't worry. We're almost there. Just as long as he doesn't leave the country. And we'll do what we can to get the rest of them. I'll be in touch."

Journey into Darkness

Chapter Thirteen

Thursday, 18th September – pm

Approaching the house with caution, Jamil was surprised to see no evidence of police presence. The road was deserted, a quiet afternoon with residents at work or busy indoors. He slipped around the side as inconspicuously as possible and peered through the glass panel of the back door. The house seemed equally deserted. He unlocked the door and stepped quietly into the kitchen, closing and locking the door behind him, creeping along the hallway and up the stairs, ready to defend himself from attack at any moment. He reached the bedroom without challenge. He changed into casual clothes, trainers, joggers and a hoodie, hanging his business clothes in the wardrobe as though he were planning to return for no doubt the house would be searched in due course. There was no paperwork to link him to the lock-up on which the rent was paid for several months more in Azad's name. As were all important documents held in the lock up to be discovered only later. But then clearly he had been followed. Their discovery would be sooner rather than later. He must make haste.

Quickly packing a bag, he left by the same way he had entered. With his passport and wallet safely in his pocket and his bank cards and both 'phones secure, he could buy a car abroad. His body was racked with shock, his heart grieving for Hasan. He made hurriedly for the lock-up, looking over his shoulder at intervals, peering anxiously at every passer-by, paranoia dogging every step. Bending at the safe, he emptied the contents into his travel bag, taking the money, all record of the bank accounts, discarding on the floor the paperwork on the apartment that was no longer secret. They would be welcome to that. He locked the safe and stood upright to steady his breath. The black plastic bags containing Katya's clothes were still where he had left them, one shoe fallen forlornly beside them onto the concrete floor and the photograph taken on their wedding day slid and lodged in the fold of one of the bags. Katya's face glowed up at him, her eyes shining with that clear light that was now haunting him. Whatever he had done to free himself of her, she followed his every move, her eyes pursuing him in his dreams and in his waking moments. The agony he was now feeling was immeasurable and though she was not present in person, through those eyes he was sure she was aware. He thrust it down into the bag out of sight. What could he do with these things now? What would be the point? He had no time. In any case, they may not be discovered until the rental period expired. maybe not even then. The landlord could simply clear his belongings and dump them. The companion chastised him.

"You fool, you should have done it before. Now you have no time."

The voices nagged him, argued against each other, rambling, incoherent, crowding out rational thought.

"It's alright. You can say she left them, that she only took some of her clothes. So you wanted them out of your sight because it was hurtful to see them there."

"It doesn't matter now," they argued. "The game is up because Jamil was careless."

"Shut up," shouted Jamil. "Shut up. What does it matter now. Leave me be."

He tried to quell a scream rising in his throat but it came out in a twisted, agonised outcry that sent him sinking to his knees. He had lost his son, his Hasan. He had lost his life. There was nothing left that was important now but survival so that one day he could return and find his boy. A new identity, a new passport. It would be possible. Disappearing in the Eastern European melting pot would not be difficult – just as long as he could get there. Pulling himself together, he stood up, brushing the dust from the floor from his joggers and prepared to leave. Turning the key in the padlock, he set off, running now, panic at his heels. Back on the main road, he hailed a taxi.

"I need to get to Dover. Quickly or I miss my crossing. Can you take me?"

"Sure, mate. Hop in."

At the terminal, he bought a ticket to Calais, relaxing a little now, more confident of his escape, waiting as calmly as he could manage with the other foot passengers to embark. A group of backpacking tourists were thronging near the exit and he mingled with them, engaging them in chit chat about their travels, moving himself further into the camouflage of the group, his hood pulled up around his head, conscious of the CCTV that would be monitoring them. As the crowd began to move forward, he moved with them, still chatting genially, still concealing himself in their centre. The ferry's engines were already running, warming in readiness to move away from the quay. They passed the point of embarkation and once aboard he disengaged himself, hurrying to the lower deck and diving into the cover of the toilets. Concealed in one of the cubicles, he waited for the movement of the ship as it pulled away. He heard the rise in volume of the engines as the ship began to move and felt the lurch as it began to turn seawards. With a sigh of relief, he left the safety of the cubicle, intent on relaxation in the coffee lounge for the remainder of the journey. But his heart was heavy. He had lost his son.

At a table by the window, he sipped his coffee on automatic pilot, staring out into the gloom of early evening. Spray from the swell of the channel was splashing up against windows clouded by condensation. The shock of the day's events was hitting him with full force now that the adrenalin level was falling and as shock gave way to reality, he felt like his heart was breaking. He felt lost, the ground from under his feet being swept away. He had no idea where he was going or why. Struggling to stabilise his emotions, he knew he had to somehow form a plan.

******

In the booth back on the quay, a member of staff was collecting together the papers now the ferry was leaving. An alert visible on his computer screen warned him of incoming mail that had lain unopened since its arrival. Casually he clicked onto it and was shocked at what confronted him.

"Christ," he muttered. "I missed it. He's on the ferry and I've let him through."

He printed it quickly and yelled to the port police, waving the paper in his hand.

"You need to stop the ferry. This guy's on the ferry and he's wanted by the Met."

"Too late, mate. She's on her way."

"But we have to do something," he insisted, aware that it was his neck that was on the line. "We have to. He's wanted for questioning for a list of crimes. Some really bad stuff."

"Are you sure it was him?"

"Positive. I noticed the scar. He'd tried to hide it under the hoodie but the hood slipped when he stooped to pick up his bag. I'm sure it's him."

"I'll get onto it. See if we can pick him up in Calais."

******

Shakespeare was apoplectic with rage.

"How the hell did this happen?" he bellowed. "It was all set up. How in God's name ... "

"They're going to try to pick him up in Calais, sir."

"They damned well better. They'd better. This is just about the last thing I wanted to hear – or wanted to tell Katya Hussein."

He picked up his phone to call Len Hutton.

"I don't believe it. Ben, what the hell happened here? They must pick him up in Calais. I'll get onto the ferry port – see what I can do. We have guys over there already dealing with the refugee problem. We'll get one of them onto it."

"Thanks for that. Let me know as soon as you hear."

"I will."

Journey into Darkness

******

On board Jamil was pulling himself together. Somehow he had
to stay free if there were any chance of him seeing Hasan
again. But first he had to get off this ferry, how to get through
the checks at the other end? They may be watching for him on
the French side.

"Maybe a lorry," he thought. "The same way we used to bring
people into Dover I can use to get into France."

He slugged back the last of the coffee, and slinging his bag
over his shoulder, he took the stairs down onto the car deck.
Wandering through the parked vehicles he came across two
lorries parked one before the other with foreign writing
emblazoned across their sides; possibly Croat, he thought, or
Serbian. Yes, they would be the best bet to try. The cabs were
empty and he settled himself to wait, crouching out of sight
between the vehicles alongside. He knew that car decks on
ferries coming into Dover were checked with dogs during the
voyage for drugs and illegals but as far as he was aware, this
did not apply on the the outward journey . But just in case, he
must be watchful. It was some time before the sound of voices
approaching caused him to hide back in the shadows. The
owners passed him by, English spoken so that he understood
the conversation.

"Should dock in about ten minutes, I would say. See you in the
cafe in Marquise."

"Ok mate, see you there."

Jamil straightened. Ten minutes. He had ten minutes to hitch
himself a ride. It was only minutes before the drivers of the
two foreign lorries appeared. They waved a farewell to each
other and opened the doors to their cabs. Jamil eyed them;
which would be the most likely, he wondered. Then making
his choice, he stepped forward. He waved a greeting to the
driver and indicated his need to speak.

"I need a lift," he began. "But out of sight. Slight brush with
an irate father. Can you give me a ride?"

The driver paused, eyeing Jamil critically.

"Where you want to go?"

"Where are you heading?"

"Prague."

"That would do me well. I'll pay well."

"How well?"

"Name your price."

The driver thought for a moment, not fooled by the man's story. He eyed Jamil quickly, the quality of his clothing, the wristwatch, the expensive baggage, the smell of expensive toiletries and the clean, manicured hands like a professional or a well-oiled criminal; no poor manual labourer this.

"On the run from the law," he guessed. "Should be worth plenty.

"£500." he said.

Jamil turned away from him and drew the money from his money belt without argument. At the sight of the money, the driver hopped down from his cab and walked around to the back of the lorry.

"Hurry," he said. "We'll be docking any minute."

In the back of the lorry, Jamil found himself ushered between boxes of computer supplies. He settled for the long journey. He was grateful he had bought water and a bar of chocolate and with the evening setting in, he would settle himself to catch some sleep once clear of the port. The driver slid down the shutter on the lorry and he heard the lock engage. It seemed an eternity until he felt the lorry ease into movement and the clunk of the wheels on the metal ramp as it left the port and crossed the boundary into the French countryside. Then the steady drone of the engine and turn of the wheels told him they were well on their way. He slumped back on the floor, trying his best to relax against the jolting but the constant drone of the engine and the discomfort of his mode of transport kept him wakeful until, finally, exhaustion overtook him and the darkness of sleep swept in.

******

It fell to Shakespeare to visit Katya and give her the news.

Helen was at her bedside on a visit when he called.

"He's left the country," he told her. "We know he left from Calais but he was missed at the other end. I'm really sorry, Katya. I think so much emphasis was put on him flying out that things were a bit sloppy at the ferry port."

Katya was distraught.

"What if he comes back? I want to leave hospital. I want to be with my son. But I can't be in that house. It's his house. I can't live there. I don't want to live there anyway. That house has bad memories for me. But with Jamil still free it would be impossible. If they missed him leaving the country they could just the same miss him if he comes back."

"No, no. I understand. You can't go back there, not with Jamil unaccounted for. I know the doctor says you're well enough to leave but I need you to stay here in the hospital until we can make other arrangements."

"But I need to be with my son. How long will this take?"

Helen intervened.

"Inspector, Katya could stay with me if that would be ok with you. And Hasan. I have spare rooms. Her husband doesn't really know me and he certainly doesn't know where I live. I don't see how he could possibly find her if she was with me. What do you think, Katya?"

Shakespeare thought for a moment.

"I don't see any problem with that. What do you think?"

"Oh, Helen. I'd be really grateful. And Hasan?"

"Someone will bring Hasan," Shakespeare agreed. "But it's a bit late now, isn't it? Best in the morning now, don't you think?"

Disappointed Katya had to agree. When Shakespeare left she and Helen packed her bags and she prepared to leave.

******

The sound of the shutter being raised brought Jamil to consciousness with a jolt. A voice shouted in the darkness.

163

"Heh. You want food?"

"Yes. Yes please. Where are we?"

"Road to Frankfurt. We at cafe. You want eat?"

"Yes. Burgers? Do they have burgers?"

"Yes. You stay. I get for you. And coffee."

"I only have English money. Ok?"

The man nodded and Jamil handed him a £10. note.

"Enough?"

Again the man nodded.

"Toilet?" asked Jamil.

"Not in there," came the reply as the man pointed to the service station. "Here," and he indicated the bushes at the lorry park boundary. Returning with the food, he gave Jamil a small battery lantern. By the dim light, Jamil ate and drank as the lorry trundled on. Replete and feeling increasingly relaxed as distance widened between himself and the channel, he turned on his side once more and slept.

Journey into Darkness

Chapter Fourteen

Friday, 19th September

Parked in the lorry park of a motorway cafe the lorry driver opened the shutters to let in a burst of autumn sunlight. Jamil winced and shielded his eyes from the sudden glare.

"You want more eat?" the driver questioned.

Jamil sidled forward to sit with his legs dangling over the tailboard. He felt stiff and confined, needing desperately to escape the confines of his prison.

"Where are we?" he asked.

"Frankfurt," came the reply.

Jamil glanced at his watch. It was 7.30 English time. He was hungry, ravenously so.

"Yes. I need breakfast."

"Ok. We clear of France now. You go. Back here in thirty minutes," and the driver tapped his watch to stress the time.

"You have Euros? You change me some money into Euros?"

The driver nodded.

Pulling money from his pocket, Jamil offered a £50. note. Conscious that he was being given a low return but with no other choice, he accepted the Euros offered, grabbed his bag and made for the buildings ahead. His mobile buzzed in his pocket.

"Allo."

"Jamil. What is happening? I have a group waiting, Can we go?"

Jamil sighed.

"No. The route is closed. I am in Europe."

There was a gasp at the other end.

"You get caught?"

"Almost."

"Where you go now?"

"I don't know yet. I'm clear of the country, that's the first thing."

"Jamil, we could do with you here. You know things. Procedures. You could help us."

"Who's us? And where's here?"

"My team. We are in Bodrum. There thousands want cross to Greece and Italy. Many Somalis. Syrians. We not even have to get them into the country, Jamil. Just put them on boats and send them in the direction they want. Greek beaches. Lampadusa island. They walk the rest. It easy money and plenty. Some make it, some not. You come? We could use you."

Jamil considered. At least it was a plan, if only for the time being.

"Ok. But it's difficult for me in Turkey. I have to use a different passport. From now on you call me Azad. And you use a different phone. I'll call you on that 'phone when I'm close."

"Ok. No problem. I'll wait for your call."

In the toilets Jamil gave the plan more thought. Once inside Turkey he could buy a car and travel down to Bodrum but he would have to be careful. The police would be watching for him in Turkey, the first place they would look. There would be lots of tourists in Bodrum to cover him; visitors for the climate and to visit Epheseus and Pamukale. The best place to hide was in a crowd. He hurried to the cafe and bought breakfast, checking his watch. 20 minutes. He still had 20 minutes. He ate a light breakfast and drank his fill of juice, then stopped at the shop to buy a bottle of water and a pack of biscuits. Making his way back to the lorry park with minutes to spare, he found that the lorry was missing from the space where he'd left it. He searched amongst the vehicles parked, looking around him, disorientated in the strangeness of his situation, from the journey and his strange, disrupted sleep.

"Where the hell ... " he began, then scanning the park again, reality dawned. The lorry was nowhere to be seen. It was gone.

"Fuck," he breathed. "He cheated me, the double-crossing bastard."

He walked dejected back to the cafe and bought more coffee, sitting at a table in the corner to rethink his plans. A train station; there must be one in Frankfurt. Or maybe he could buy a car here but that could be too risky. He would have to produce documents and draw money from Azad's bank account.

"Your bank account," he reminded himself. "You are Azad Dalman now. No problem."

But it will have to be by train from here. He could go through Hungary and Romania, then down through Bulgaria to the Turkish border. It would take time but once there he knew enough ways and means to avoid detection and the best places to cross. He walked to the information desk in the foyer.

"You speak English?" he asked.

The girl nodded.

"My car has broken down," he began. "I need to get to the train station in Frankfurt. Is there a taxi service anywhere?"

The girl nodded again and handed him a business card with a 'phone number.

"You call," she told him. "They will come."

Several days later

It was days later that he crossed the northern Turkish border undetected and in anonymity at a point where he knew the border to be porous. He had grown a beard which he thought would help to conceal his identity but the scar tissue on his neck prevented the growth of hair and seemed to him to make the abhorrence even more apparent. The funds in his pocket were dwindling fast. Reluctant to use his bank card to draw funds from an account that could be monitored, he hitched ride after ride southwards through the country, eating and sleeping in greasy spoon cafés and cheap hotels until at last the southern coastline was in sight. He took Azad's phone from his pocket and called.

"Ahmet, this is Azad. I am almost here."

"Good. I will send someone to fetch you. Where are you?"

He gave directions to the roadside cafe north of the town where his latest lorry ride had dropped him.

"Deniz will fetch you. Wait there. Have coffee or something. Will take him maybe half an hour. Is good to be back in the country, heh, Jamil?"

"Azad. The name's Azad."

"Yes, sorry. Ok. See you later."

The ride into town when Deniz arrived was surreal. The tension now relieved Jamil could relax and reassess the state his life was now in. He could hardly believe the events that had uprooted him in so short a time and his grief at losing Hasan hit him again and again each time he stood still. Deniz's attempts at conversation were unbearable and eventually ceased when met by no more than grunts and sighs. In his need to numb the pain, Jamil buried his emotions beneath an avalanche of activity once Deniz left him at a house on the wooded hillside.

"Ahmet say you make yourself at home. Have a shower, make yourself a meal. He is busy now with today's shipment. He will be back shortly, as soon as the boats have left."

Jamil busied himself while he waited. He showered and shaved away the dust and grime of his journey and the beard he had grown. In the kitchen, he loaded his soiled clothing into the washing machine and dumped bits of rubbish he had accumulated in his pockets into the bin. The resumption of some kind of order to his existence gave him comfort, the misconception of his life restored. Checking the 'fridge and cupboards, he abandoned any intention of making a meal, his former healthy appetite replaced by a constant feeling of nausea. Coffee had become his staple diet.

When Ahmet arrived, Jamil threw himself into the practicalities of the environment that was now his home and lifestyle – at least for the foreseeable future. He needed time to stabilise, to reassess his direction for the future.

"Heh, Azad. Welcome. Welcome back to your home country. You must feel pretty good to be back, huh?"

Jamil had little to say. Was this his home country? How could it be when the most important person in his life was back in his old life, in the country and environment he had called home for many years. He dismissed Ahmet's question with several of his own.

"It is strange, Ahmet. Different. So what is the set-up here and what do you think I can do? What's in it for me?"

Submerging his pain beneath a veneer of calm, Jamil adopted the persona of man of the world, so the two men talked jovially, then haggled, then agreed terms of a partnership that would serve them both.

"I need a car."

"No problem. We have several. You use one until you've organised one of your own. They are old. Don't attract attention. We don't spend much money round here. Keep a low profile. We save the flashy lifestyle for when we fly to Istanbul."

"The local police. Are they .. ah, friendly?"

"We have a contact. But like I say, we keep a low profile. Don't give them any reason to take a closer look. Common sense, heh?"

"Of course."

The winter months were a quiet time, the waters too dangerous for many to attempt the crossing. Only the hardiest and most desperate thronged to the shore for their services. Lying low Jamil attracted no attention from the authorities as he and Ahmet prepared for the coming avalanche of refugees in spring. He submerged himself to excess in the local community, in wine, women and song, anything to blot out the pain of losses that were ever with him, optimistic that the warmth and sunshine of summer would help to heal his

169

wounds. He would make money. He would buy himself a new identity and have cosmetic surgery to reduce the scar on his neck. One day he would return to England and look for his son.

As winter gave way to spring, the season began in earnest. It was on one such morning that Jamil found himself confronted once more by the demons in his head.

At a secluded beach outside the tourist sweep, Ahmet was herding a crowd of refugees onto a boat at the rough, wooden jetty. His mood was less jovial than usual, a little sour from a hangover. He was rougher than he needed to be, shoving people forward in his impatience and desire to return to his bed.

"Come on. Hurry, hurry. Move on."

A woman in the melee lost her footing as she endeavoured to complete the manoeuvre from the jetty onto the boat. In her arms she carried a small child, a boy with round dark eyes like saucers and hair as dark as pitch. In a frightening moment the boy slid from her grasp in danger of disappearing through the gap between terra firma and the boat to fall into the water. Without hesitation , Jamil lunged forward to grasp the boy and steady the mother.

"Hasan," he murmured. "Hasan."

Back steady on her feet, with her child replaced firmly in her grasp, the mother looked intently into Jamil's eyes.

"Shukran," she told him quietly. "Shukran." Thank you.

Without a word he nodded calmly, but inside he was shaking. The boy was about the age that Hasan would be now, the mother's face as gentle as Katya.

"Hurry, Azad," shouted Ahmet. "Hurry. We will miss the tide."

Jamil was angered.

"What's your hurry Ahmet. We have time. You need to be more careful, huh?"

Jamil waved on the last of the boatload and raised the gangway, preparing to launch the boat seaward. But he was working on automatic pilot, unable to rationalise what was happening around him for the pain inside him was all consuming, the return of his sorrow overwhelming him like the waves that were rocking the boat. Guilt was rearing its head, an emotion unfamiliar in recent times and in its wake, all thought of the future was swept away.

******

Ben Shakespeare expressed his frustration.

"I can't believe that in all these months he's not touched the bank account or used either of the mobile numbers we have. He must have access to facilities through other people. Or he's earning money so he doesn't need it. "

"He'll have picked up a new 'phone without difficulty, sir. Easy enough."

"Yes, you're right."

Shakespeare sighed.

"Get on to the Turkish police again, Mickey. Give them a nudge. I suspect they consider it low priority. See if you can prompt them into action."

"I'll try, sir; but last time I spoke to them they were a bit dismissive. They said they were doing their best but they had more pressing matters to deal with. They said they'd visited his home village but no-one there had seen him. The couple who cared for him after his mother died were quite distressed to hear what he is accused of but they promised to get in touch with the police if he turns up there. So the police left it there. Like I said, they said they had more important things to deal with."

"I'm sure they do. They have big problems with refugees on their own borders, what with all the trouble in Syria. Jamil Hussein is small fry by their standards. But it galls me to let it drift. And for Katya Hussein it's a constant anxiety."

171

Mickey was thoughtful.

"I spoke to her the other evening. I had supper with her at Helen's. She's getting on with life and doing really well but she's very security nervous. She said she feels like she's watching over her shoulder all the time – afraid of him just turning up and trying to snatch Hasan again. And if he did, of course, he could kill or injure her and be out of the country with the boy before anyone even knew. I tried to reassure her that he'd have quite a job finding her now,. She's moved to a completely different area and reverted to her maiden name. Hopefully we'd know he was back in the country before he had chance to find her. Now the locks are changed on that house and a security alarm installed he couldn't access anything there. Not that we found anything ourselves that he'd want. But if he tried to get in the alarm would alert us."

"Let's hope so. He'd come back under a new alias and somewhere under the radar. He's a man with resources and contacts."

"But does he even know she's alive, sir? How would he know?"

"Hopefully he doesn't, Mickey. Hopefully not."

"Given what we know about his activities here, sir, he'll have gone underground amongst the criminal fraternity, won't he? So he's likely to be down south somewhere – near the Syrian border where the main of the refugees are."

"Of course. He clearly had contacts in the country so I wouldn't mind betting that he's actively involved with the trafficking gangs there. Which is probably why he doesn't need the funds in those bank accounts. He'll be making a mint. Maybe a trip to Turkey for us would be the best way to proceed. With the co-operation of the Turkish authorities, of course. I'll speak to the Chief Super. See if we can fit it in between our current cases. Find out from the Turkish chaps where they believe the main of the trafficking gangs are based and if they're willing to assign an officer to work with us on this. And I'll set it up from there."

As Mickey left his office, Shakespeare's 'phone rang. It was the officer on reception calling.

"Sir, there's a young lady here asking to see you. Says her name is Lauren? Didn't give a surname. She says you'll just know Lauren."

Shakespeare was surprised.

"Yes, I do. Ok, well bring her up."

As she entered his office, he rose from behind the desk and walked to meet her, hand outstretched in greeting.

"Hello, Lauren. This is a nice surprise. How are you?"

"I'm good, Mr Shakespeare, thank you. Really good."

"Please, have a seat. You're looking really well, I must say. So – how's life with you these days."

"It's really good, thank you. An' I just wanted to tell you that it's all thanks to you."

"Oh, I don't know about that, Lauren. I'm sure it's all about you really."

"Well, if you hadn't helped me like you did I wouldn't've 'ad the chance, would I? Like – the other girls, they got done, didn't they? Immoral earnings and that. But you didn't do that to me."

"Well, the other girls were older, Lauren. They could have done other things with their life if they'd tried but they didn't. So what's happening with you?"

"I've got a place at college. Art. Like my teachers always said. The people at the hostel – they helped me."

"That's great news. I'm sure you'll make a success of it. Are you still at the hostel?"

"For the time being but they're gonna help me get a place with someone. Assisted livin', they call it. I think they'd like my room back for someone else soon. Someone else who needs it like I did. But what I really came to tell you is that they helped me find my Dad. An' he's being really supportive. I was really nervous when I contacted him. Thought he might not want to know me. But he was really pleased and we met. We've met several times since. He didn't know I'd left Mum an' he's really sorry for not being there for me. An' I've got a half sister called Emily."

Shakespeare nodded as he listened, delighted in the change from the vulnerable girl he had first met to the bubbly young woman now before him.

"We've found my Mum too. She's been in an' out of rehab." Lauren grimaced.

" She's not doin' very well but she's tryin'."

"Kicking the habit is really hard, Lauren. It will take a lot of time and effort and she'll probably relapse from time to time along the way. But like you say - at least she's trying."

"Social Services are helpin'. I went to see her. She cried and cried and hugged me 'till it made me ache. I felt sorry for her."

"Are you going to see her again?"

"Yes. I'll keep in touch – with both of them, Mum and Dad."

"But you're not going to live with them?"

"No. I'm staying here – in London. The college I'm going to is here and I've made some friends now. They're good people – not like Sadie and that lot."

"Well, there are some really bad people in this world, Lauren – but there are more good people than bad. At least, that's what I believe."

"I think so, too. Thank you for helping me, Mr Shakespeare."

"Thank you for coming to tell me, Lauren. I wish you all the very best."

Journey into Darkness

Chapter Fifteen

Where from here?

"Heh, Azad. Let's go. Come on. Turn us around. Let's go."

"Ahmet, their boat is letting in water. It's sinking already. They can't swim, these people. If we leave them they will drown. All of them. Like the ones before."

Ahmet shouted impatiently and in anger.

"What, you have a conscience suddenly? What's wrong with you? You think they are the first? You know not. What would they go back to? Murder by IS? Rape? Abuse? At least this way they have a chance. And if they don't make it, better a watery grave than what they've left behind. Look, Jamil, we didn't make this situation. We didn't cause the war in Syria. We didn't invade Iraq. We didn't get rid of Gaddafi. We're not in IS; we're not even Muslim. We just give these people what they want – huh? Stop moaning and get on with the job."

"You mean a watery grave? Is that what they want? They are given boats that are not seaworthy. There's no way that rusty old heap is going to get them across to the Greek mainland. We are paid enough to get better boats, Ahmet. That's your part of the operation. In the boats you give them they have no chance; no chance at all."

"I get the boats at a good price. And I'm told they are good. So not my problem if they don't make it."

"But you know that's not true, Ahmet. You know it's not true."

"So suddenly it worries you then, Jamil. Suddenly. Then go join them, Jamil. Azad. Whoever you are. Go join them. Go. I don't need a partner like you," and with a sudden and violent shove, Ahmet pushed Jamil hard so that he lost his footing and toppled over the side of the boat into the sea. Taken by surprise, Jamil sank beneath the waves, then fought against the water to break above the surface. Gasping he thrashed about in the water, turning himself in his disorientation to redirect himself back towards the boat, shouting at Ahmet to wait. But Ahmet turned away already firing up the engine.

175

"Ahmet, no," shouted Deniz and he lunged forward, cutting the engine back, then holding his arm out to Jamil who, a weak swimmer held back by water-logged clothing, was struggling to reach them in the water.

"Come, Jamil. Come," he called holding out his arm and he helped Jamil heave himself up back up over the side, back onto the deck where he crashed face down, a coughing, spluttering mess of clothing saturated in sea water.

"You crazy, man. You crazy," Deniz shouted at Ahmet. "Why turn on him, for God's sake."

Ahmet turned away, shrugging, unrepentant of his behaviour and surprised by the ferocity of Deniz's reaction. Snatching the wheel of the power boat Deniz took control and turned it back towards Bodrum. Sitting up and taking off his water-filled trainers, Jamil breathed deeply. It was clear the partnership was falling apart.

The last six months had been hell on earth, crimes worse than anything he would have imagined himself capable of. Thousands of people condemned to death at sea or to degradation so far removed from what he and his fellow traffickers had promised, all semblance of integrity abandoned. His pockets bulged with money that gave him no pleasure. All appetite for the trappings of success abandoned, he drove a beaten old Ford and lived in a grubby apartment block overlooking the very sea shore he abused daily. His heart and soul were black with despair.

Back in his apartment, he stripped out of his wet clothing and looked at himself in the mirror, unshaven, unkempt, shaken from the morning's events that haunted his soul. They had watched the boat heading across the choppy spring waters of the Aegean, he and the rest of the gang. Already the boat was low in the water. He could only imagine the fate that lay ahead. Each day on the tv the news pictures told the story in graphic detail, showed the anguished faces of the few survivors rescued by the Greek and Italian authorities; mothers who watched a much loved child sink slowly beneath the waters as they were forced to choose between their progeny, an attempted rescue of the child sinking in the water or the safety of the babe in their arms. It was no choice at all. Small children were screaming and starving; old people weeping and distraught. Every baby was Hasan, every mother Katya, every young girl he heard or saw raped became Sofiya, every old woman his mother and his aunt. And him - his life had become a hell on earth, a life crushed beneath the weight of his guilt for his crimes. He had had a good life but he had abused it, degraded it to come to this. The grief he felt at losing Hasan was with him every moment, the abhorrence of his treatment of a loving, trusting wife. Self-recrimination dogged his every move. And more.

He had learned so much in recent months that he had denied before, of gypsies who were not really gypsies at all but people displaced through no fault of their own, a teeming humanity whose lives had been ripped apart by war and famine and persecution, fleeing in terror and risking all for a better life. And he abused them daily. Of women who were not scheming and out to get you but merely human beings who would sacrifice all for the sake of their children and their loved ones. And he had abused them too. And just as his arrogance, his anger and hatred and the crimes he had committed had set him outside of the community he had lived in with Katya so now this new awareness and understanding set him apart from those around him who would draw him deeper into their brutal world of revilement. He belonged nowhere and to no-one, especially not to the likes of Ahmet. Standing alone and seeing before him the man he had become, knowing the life he now led and hated with every fibre of his being, he made a decision. He showered; he shaved; he dressed in clean, pressed clothes until at least his outward appearance was one of respectability. He packed a bag with clean clothing and the barest of necessities, then shoved the wads of money into the pockets of his jeans, tucked both passports into his pocket, picked up his car key and

177

left the building.

He called at a local car dealer and upgraded his car; nothing fancy but in good enough order to stand up to the journey he intended. Keeping back enough money for food and drink and petrol, he called at the local bank and deposited the remainder in Azad's bank account. Then he opened an account in the name of Jamil Hussein and transferred the funds from Azad's account across. It no longer mattered if the authorities were watching; it was over anyway. After a last coffee at a local restaurant where his activities were unknown and he was welcomed, he bought a carton of juice and a baguette for the journey and set off in the direction of what had once been his home. His stomach was churning at what he knew was a last goodbye. The sun was glinting on the blue, blue waters of the sea as he drove along the front towards the main road out of town. The first of the season's tourists were already settling themselves on the beach in their swimsuits and bikinis, smoothing sun block onto bodies pale from the European winter. With one last look, he steered northwards and inland with resolve. His mind was set.

Booking into a modest hotel for the night, he bought a pen and a pad of notepaper and envelopes. He had tried to eat in a cafe but his appetite again deserted him and he stirred the food around on the platter before abandoning the task completely. His mind was intent on the task ahead. Returning to his room, he sat for some time with the paper and pen before him but inspiration eluded him and eventually he sank into sleep without achievement. The rising sun was his alarm clock and once more, he showered and shaved, dressed himself in clean, pressed clothing and headed for the cafe for coffee. He had no desire for food, ignoring the breakfast menu, opting only to buy a bottle of water and a roll to take away which he wrapped in a napkin and tucked in his bag. Leaving with a wave of parting to the girl at the desk, he turned the car towards the village of his birth. Within him was a total calm.

Old Adalet saw him approach from where he sat on the bench outside the bakery, his morning work now done. The call to prayer was loudspeakered from the mosque outside the village, the sing song tones floating through the air above their heads. Looking upwards from his place on the bench, Adalet mopped his weather-beaten brow with his apron and screwed up his eyes against the sun, shielding them from the glaring light with his hands.

"Well, Jamil. I thought we might see you."

"How are you, Adalet?"

"Better than you, I think. They have been here looking for you, Jamil. The police. Bad things they've told us about you."

"What things have they said?"

"That you tried to murder your wife. Is this true, Jamil?"

"Who told them this?"

"She told them."

"My wife?"

"Yes. Your wife. If you meant to kill her then you failed. She lives and has told them this. Is it true, Jamil?"

Jamil was shocked. How many more shocks did life hold in store for him. And yet he was glad that she lived. At least now Hasan had his mother. At least it was one less death on his conscience, even though he had tried. It no longer mattered that people knew; it was simply what he deserved. And he knew now why he could not kill her himself as he had done with others, why he had hired a hitman. Because after all he had loved her, as he had once loved his mother, an emotion he had denied to himself since Meryam. The recognition stripped away the last shreds of deception.

"Yes. It is true, Adalet. I'm a guilty man. But I'm glad she lives. I'm glad I failed."

Adalet stared at him steadily, weighing up his next words carefully.

"And what of your mother, Jamil? Your aunt? What of them?"

Adalet's eyes told Jamil of the old man's suspicions.

"Yes. Them too. I started the fire."

"Yes. I always wondered. There was something about you that gave it away but I could never quite grasp it. Nesrin, she said no. She cared for you like one of her own, like a mother hen. She would not hear of it. Not Jamil, she would say. He's just disturbed by the tragedy, by all the abuse. But me - I always wondered."

A calm, quiet rested between the two men as they regarded each other.

"Come. Sit with me a moment, Jamil. Tell me – what are you going to do?"

Jamil sat on the bench next to Adalet, a deep affection for this kind old man washing over him. He felt ashamed of his neglect since leaving the village. He had owed them the debt of his life and education, Adalet and Nesrin, but he had never acknowledged it until now.

"There will be no more, Adalet. I promise you. I have done bad things and I must pay the price. I have lost the son I loved and abused the wife I should have valued. I was crazy. I think all my life I've been crazy. I'm not crazy any more. There is nothing more in life for me without justice."

"Well, a man has to come to recognise himself for what he is and the things he has done by himself. Other people telling you has no effect unless it's what you want to believe. Until we accept ourselves we can't truly accept others. We all struggle with facing up to our faults sometimes, our wrongdoings."

"I can't imagine you having any, Adalet."

"Oh, Jamil. I am not a saint. Sometimes I'm impatient when I shouldn't be, hard on people when I should be tolerant and understanding. We all have faults, Jamil. Accepting those faults is not always easy."

"But those things are nothing, Adalet, to the things I have done."

"No, but they can be at the root of our problems. Intolerance. Prejudice. Ignorance even. Now you've reached the point of recognising where it all went wrong for you, you can begin achieving salvation. But it has to start inside of you. Why do you think you did these things, Jamil?"

"I wanted control, Adalet. I wanted to control everyone around me. My wife. My son. If Katya didn't do what I wanted ….. I felt a deep anger. A rejection. And I wanted money. To be a big man so that everyone would say, heh – that Jamil, he's really someone . So now I have money but the way I earned that money … I am ashamed."

Jamil paused, silent and retrospective. Adalet broke the silence for them both.

"What do you see, Jamil - when you look inside yourself?"

"A sinner."

"But a repentant one."

"Yes."

"Good. Then your soul will be cleansed and once you have paid your debt to those you've harmed then you will have the chance to restore a life for yourself. A life worth living."

"After my mother, my aunt? After Katya? I don't think so."

"Jamil, you were a child; an abused child. You could not have understood then the implications of what you did. The nightmares you suffered when you were with us told us that. And your wife? Well, she lives and you are repentant. You'll go to prison. But after …. "

Jamil said nothing. He could not tell Adalet the extent of his crimes, his shame was too great. He could not tell him about Meryam and about all the people since. He believed his crimes to be too great to ever hope for redemption.

"Where do you go now?"

"Where I need, Adalet. Where I must."

Adalet laid his hand gently on Jamil's arm.

"Then God go with you. And remember; God forgives all who truly repent."

Jamil looked into the old man's eyes and saw the love there he had failed to see before and for one more time he understood it.

"Give my best to Nesrin," he said. "Tell her thank you. And

that I'm sorry."
"I will."

Jamil walked to the lake, his favourite spot, the place where his downfall had begun on the night he set the fire that had killed his mother and his aunt. Like the air around him, his heart was heavy, laden with the expectant calm that came before the storm. Sitting on a grassy mound, he took the pen and paper he had brought from the car and began to write. The words flowed unhindered from his pen onto paper. He wrote two letters; one to the police and one to Katya. As he wrote them, the tears flowed just as freely and the pain in his heart was overwhelming. His head hurt and he wanted to stop but he knew he must say it all. When he was done, he walked back to his car and placed the letters on the dashboard. Then taking a length of rope from the boot where he had placed it, he locked the car, put the keys in his pocket and walked back to the lakeside. He surrendered to the darkness.

******

The alarm went up as the two boys rushed into the village, arms and legs animated, shouting for their father with voices raised in shock and anguish. Villagers came rushing from every sidestreet and open doorway to meet them in their panic.
"What is it? What's wrong?"
"Baba. Baba. There's a man. By the lake. He's hanging from a tree."

******

With Hasan in her arms, Katya answered the knock at the door to find Shakespeare and Gray on the doorstep.
"Hello, Katya. May we come in?"
"Of course. I'm surprised to see you. I'm just making coffee. Would you like some?"

"That would be lovely. Yes. I'm sorry it's been a little while. It doesn't mean we haven't been busy though. And we felt you were doing alright once you moved into the flat; that you were getting your life sorted so we didn't want to intrude on that. You're doing well, I think."

The two detectives seated themselves at the table in the tiny kitchen. Katya could not wait to ask the question?

"Have you come with news?"

"We have. Let's have the coffee and sit comfortably. And Hasan, he's a busy chap now, by the look of him."

"Oh, yes. Crawling everywhere and climbing now; on the chairs, on the sofa. I have to watch him all the time. He will be walking any day and tomorrow is his birthday."

She lifted Hasan and sat him in his high chair, taking a biscuit from a packet in the cupboard and placing it in his hand.

"That will keep him busy for a moment. He is due his sleep soon so I can put him to bed if we need to talk."

She placed the cups and saucers on a tray with a percolator of fresh coffee and the milk and sugar.

"Let me," Mickey insisted, rising from his seat to take the tray from her. They settled at the table and Katya looked at them expectantly for whatever news they were bringing her.

"As I'm sure you're expecting, Katya, it's about Jamil," Shakespeare began. "He's been found."

Katya nodded and smiled nervously.

"In this country?"

"No. In Turkey."

She let out a sigh of relief.

"Thank God," she breathed. "I was so afraid you were going to tell me that he is back. That he would be looking for us."

"That won't happen now. Katya, Jamil is dead."

The shock winded her for a moment.

"How?"

It was all she could manage to say.

"He hung himself."

"Oh."

Her hand went to her mouth and tears welled in her eyes. A cocktail of emotions swirled inside her, the shock and sadness defusing the anger, the desire for revenge that had been her constant companion these many months. She had wanted justice, she had wanted him to pay but she had never wished him dead and not like this. The memory of the tormented man waking from his nightmares became uppermost in her mind. Yes, he had always been just one step ahead of self-destruct – until now. Shakespeare gave her a moment to gather herself. Hasan was lolling in his high chair, clearly ready for sleep.

"Look, why don't you put Hasan to bed and then we can talk." She nodded and lifting her son from his chair, disappeared from the room.

On her return, she was calmer and ready now to hear all she needed to know.

"His crimes were many, Katya. He left two letters, one for the police and one for you; both in Turkish. We had the one translated, I have brought the other one for you. And I've asked Helen to come and stay with you while you read it. Is that ok?" Katya nodded.

"Tell me what you know," she asked.

"It seems that Jamil's troubles began in childhood. We've learned from the couple who brought him up after his mother died that his mother and her sister would beat him regularly and he was subjected to constant verbal abuse. Not that that excuses his crimes. Many people are abused but they don't all become murderers or abusers themselves, though some do. And then, just as many who've had perfectly happy untroubled childhoods turn bad. Who knows why? But for Jamil it was the beginning. So he killed them. That is, he set the fire that killed them. He was a child and if his crime had been detected then things might have turned out differently for him and for his future. But I suppose the fact that he got away with it coloured his thinking. He must have thought himself immune, above the law."

The tears came and Katya hung her head, not wanting them to

see..

"He never said; only that his family were all dead but not how. He would never talk about it. I never pushed him because I know what it is like to lose all the family you have. I have too. But I understand now why he would never say. And the nightmares."

Shakespeare continued.

"Then there was a girl. Meryam. She spurned him; rejected what he saw as his first love. So he killed her too. He was 15."

Katya winced. Shakespeare paused.

"Are you alright? Do you want me to go on?"

She nodded, unable to speak.

"He admits to the trafficking of illegal immigrants into this country. I think it just started with turning a blind eye here and there for a bribe, then escalated into a full scale operation. When he fled from here he became involved in trafficking in Turkey. Boat loads of refugees. I'm sure you've seen it all on the news. But it sickened him. At last some sort of conscience kicked in and he felt he couldn't go on. He did make some reparation though. He left names, places; and mobile phones in the car with their passwords. That's going to keep police on both sides of the channel busy for a while. And with you, he admits to attempting to get rid of you to keep Hasan, a matter he came to regret. He wanted just the two of them."

"Yes. His love for Hasan was .. how do you say?"

"Obsessional?"

"Yes, obsessional."

"He says in his letter that you should have been the best thing that could have happened in his life, that he was crazy not to see it but now he is not. He says he is sorry. But I'm sure he will tell you all you need to know in the letter he's left for you. When you've read it, do you mind if we ask you more questions? There may be more in it that we need to know."

Katya nodded. A knock on the door paused the conversation as Helen arrived.

"We're going to leave you now, Katya – and come back to see you tomorrow. When you've had time to take all this in. The shock is too much at the moment. Then we can talk about practical things. He has left all his money in an account for you and Hasan and willed the house to you."

"I don't want it. None of it. It's dirty money. I don't want it. Hasan and me, we are fine now. I am getting my life back together – work and nursery for Hasan. And I have good friends to help me. I don't want his dirty money"

"Well, the authorities will confiscate some of the money anyway, but it's too soon for you to make that decision. Try to remember that some things were bought with his salary. The house …. "

He paused.

"You need to be practical about it for both of you. So we'll leave you now and call again tomorrow."

Katya saw him to the door and watched as Shakespeare walked towards his car.

"Come on, Mickey," he called over his shoulder. "No fraternising in work hours. Duty calls."

Walking with Helen to the doorway, Mickey bid the two women goodbye.

"He's a good man, DCI Shakespeare," said Helen.

"Yes, he is. I like working for him."

Mickey grinned.

"Has he quoted Shakespeare at you yet?"

"No!"

"He will. Oh, he will."

"Well, you'll just have to sing him some Mumford and Sons then," and with a smile shared between them, he followed Shakespeare to the car, singing as he went.

Roll away your stone, I'll roll away mine
Together we can see what we will find
Don't leave me alone at this time
For I'm afraid of what I will discover inside

Journey into Darkness

With a turn, a jaunty wave of the hand and a broad grin, he was gone.

Hasan was still sleeping and the women had time to talk. Between her tears, Katya unburdened everything that Shakespeare had told her.

"Shall I make us fresh coffee while you read your letter, Katya?"

Katya's hands were shaking as she tore open the envelope. Jamil's writing began neatly, orderly, as if he had been in control and intent on saying all he needed to tell her. But as he wrote on, it became less so and here and there the ink had smudged a little, the paper watermarked and she thought he must have written it by the lake where they had found him or maybe in the rain. And then it occurred to her; perhaps he had been crying. He told her how he regretted the way he had treated her, of the things he had come to understand and that now he knew he had loved her, that he had learned what love truly was and that she had been a loving wife and mother so undeserving of all he had done.

> *"I know you will take good care of Hasan and with you he will grow up to be a fine young man, not like his father. I do not deserve life itself for the things I have done, not the space on God's earth or the clean, fresh air I am stealing from those more worthy. I only pray that when you tell Hasan of me you will find it in your heart to be kindly and to tell him that, whatever I did, what ever I was, I loved him, I loved you both. Forgive me, Katya, if you can and find the happiness in your life you deserve."*

As she read her heart was breaking, for here in his letter was the man she had once believed Jamil could be. He had been damaged too, a broken soul just as she had once been damaged by life's trouble and trickery, just like her Pippa. In the end he had overcome but too late - for now that man was gone.

******

Helen put her arm around her friend's shoulder.

"Are you alright?"

"Yes. Yes, I am alright. It is sad, Helen, but it is … what do the Americans call it? Closure? After all that he did to hurt me, after all the fear and worry of his coming back to cause more pain, it is over."

"Yes. I'm glad for you. And we are here to help you, your friends."

They talked for a short time before Helen rose to leave.

"Katya, I have to go back to work but you're still coming for supper tomorrow, aren't you? And Hasan. We'll celebrate his birthday."

Katya nodded, dabbing her eyes with a tissue and doing her best to compose herself.

"Would you like me to ring Martin? He isn't on duty today. He could come."

Katya shook her head.

"Not just now, Helen. I need a little time on my own. Just me and Hasan. Despite all that he did, I feel grief for Jamil's death. We were good once. We could have been good again – if only ….."

"I understand. Are you sure you'll be alright?"

"Yes. I'm sure. But if I need him, I'll call Martin and ask him to come. He is coming in the morning anyway."

"He loves you, Katya. You know that, don't you?"

"Yes. And I him, I think. But it has been so complicated until now. Always wondering if Jamil will appear. Always checking each time I leave the flat in case he has found us; always over the shoulder. And I loved him once - before I lost him."

"Well, that's all over now. In a little while, when you've recovered from the shock of all that you've learned and the sadness you now feel at Jamil's end - then you'll be free. To

188

choose how you want to live. A whole new beginning. Try to keep focused on that. I'll call you in the morning but if you need me in the meantime, call. I can come when I've finished work . I mean it. Don't be alone when you don't need to be. If not we'll speak in the morning and I'll see you tomorrow evening. And Martin. And Mickey Gray's coming, too."
Katya brightened.
"Ah. A new admirer for you, Helen?"
Helen smiled.
"Well, it's early days but … mmm, maybe. We met out for a drink the other evening, just the two of us. The first time; it's always been meeting with you and Martin until now. And he's taking me to a concert next week. Mumford and Sons. I like them; they're a good band."

******

As they drove back to the station, Shakespeare and Mickey talked over the meeting and the news they had imparted
"I'd have liked to bring him to justice. The policeman in me wanted it. Seems to me he cheated the system. But in terms of humanity, well, he was clearly a greatly disturbed individual. Such a waste. Of a life; of lives; of all that potential."
"But we've achieved more arrests and broken up a trafficking ring; that wouldn't have happened if he hadn't taken this option, would it? Would he have admitted anything if he'd been faced with prison?"
"That's true enough, Mickey. You're right. And for Katya it's no doubt the best outcome in the long run. Make a note, will you? When we come tomorrow we must bring a card and a present for Hasan. Now, I think it's a down the 'pub night tonight, don't you?"
"Sounds good to me, sir."
"Right then. Ring the team and tell them to meet us at the 'pub. And I'll get Daniel to join us."
"Daniel?"

"My son, Sergeant And by the way, he tells me Mumford and Sons are a good band so you'll no doubt have a bit to talk about."

"Oh, good. Pity we didn't get our trip to Turkey, though, sir. I was quite looking forward to that – all that sun, sea and sand. I've never been to Turkey."

Shakespeare answered wryly.

"It wasn't going to be a jolly, Sargeant. We would have been going to work. And the places we would have been going to are no picnic right now."

Mickey grinned.

"But just a quick trip to the beach surely. A dip in the sea? Once we'd caught him, of course," he added solemnly.

"Your optimism does you credit, Mickey."

Before he could say another word, Shakespeare's mobile buzzed. He tapped onto hands free and paused with anticipation. With the conversation ended he gave Mickey the news.

"Right, Mickey. Duty calls. Suspicious death at Westminster; that should be an interesting one. Better get there before the press ratpack descend, if they're not there already. How the hell they get to know these things so quickly beats me."

In a cheerful voice Shakespeare launched into prose:

"Once more unto the breach, dear friends, once more;
Or close up the wall with our English dead.
Cry 'God for Harry, England and Saint George!'"

"That's an abridged version, Sergeant There's a bit more to it than that."

"Yes, sir. I'm sure there is. But it's enough for me, thanks all the same."

'Human trafficking is an open wound on the body of contemporary society, a scourge upon the body of Christ. It is a crime against humanity.' Pope Francis, April 2014

Journey into Darkness

Made in the USA
Charleston, SC
26 August 2015